F.

DOCTOR·WHO

The Krillitane Storm

Medieval etching (c.AD 1140)

DOCTOR·WHO

The
Krillitane
Storm

CHRISTOPHER COOPER

BOOKS

2 4 6 8 10 9 7 5 3

Published in 2009 by BBC Books, an imprint of Ebury Publishing
A Random House Group Company

Doctor Who is a BBC Wales production for BBC One
Executive Producers: Russell T Davies and Julie Gardner

Original series broadcast on BBC Television. Format © BBC 1963.
'Doctor Who', 'TARDIS' and the Doctor Who logo are trademarks of the
British Broadcasting Corporation and are used under licence.
Krillitanes created by Toby Whithouse.

The Random House Group Ltd Reg. No. 954009.
Addresses for companies within the Random House Group can be found
at www.randomhouse.co.uk.

A CIP catalogue record for this book is available from the British Library.

ISBN 978 1 846 07761 6

The Random House Group Limited supports the Forest Stewardship
Council (FSC), the leading international forest certification organisation.
All our titles that are printed on Greenpeace approved FSC certified
paper carry the FSC logo. Our paper procurement policy can be found
at www.rbooks.co.uk/environment

Series Consultant: Justin Richards
Project Editor: Steve Tribe
Cover design by Lee Binding © BBC 2009

Typeset in Albertina and Deviant Strain
Printed and bound in Germany by GGP Media GmbH

For Jo

Brother Neame lay still where he'd fallen, conscious that any hint of movement might reveal his hiding place. He fought to stifle the desperate urge to suck in lungfuls of air, each breath roaring in his ears as if screaming, 'Over here.'

With the passing of each agonising moment, he could feel the dampness of the sodden grass, soaking through his robes until it met his trembling body, the icy chill flooding over his skin with such ferocity that his pounding heart could do little to fight it.

Yet the monk remained still, listening desperately for any sign of pursuit.

The coming dawn would see a deep frost spread across the county like a cotton shroud. How beautiful it would be. Crisp, white, clean. Would he live to see that morning? Or would the Devil take him first?

Silence.

Neame lay there for a moment longer, exhausted. The pain in his ankle was excruciating. He must have twisted it as he fell. Would it still bear his weight? Could he still run?

The horse was dead, of course. It could not have survived the attack just moments before, from whatever it was that had sprung out of the night, like the Devil incarnate, sweeping the doomed animal from the track and into the darkness in a mess of limbs, out of sight. Neame shuddered at the recollection – the horse's terrified whinnying followed by the crack of bones, snapping like dry wood.

Then came the roar, the sound of the Devil himself: a scream that ripped through the air from the depths of Hell itself; a noise not of God's creation. And Brother Neame had fled into the night.

Tentatively lifting his head, Neame could make out the reassuring tower of the Cathedral in the distance, silhouetted against the heavy clouds, standing tall above Worcester's rooftops, a vision of hope.

The town was so close. Even with his injured ankle he could make the distance, he felt sure of it. All he had to do was get close enough to scream for assistance, and help would come. Even in these dark times, help would come. Wouldn't it?

One thing was for certain, he couldn't stay lying in this muddy field. If the Devil didn't get him, then the bitter winter cold certainly would.

Gathering his last reserves of energy, Brother Neame made a run for it.

Pain seared instantly through his leg, his ankle threatening to buckle beneath him. Neame gritted his teeth and carried on, limping badly, fighting back a wave of nausea. His single thought was to reach the city gate. The fear drove him on, running, running, resisting the urge to look back.

When it came, the force of the impact was as powerful as it was unexpected, and for a few moments Neame couldn't move from the shock. Shaking his head to clear it, the monk struggled to his feet, spinning around in search of his assailant, but there was nothing.

Absently, his gaze fell upon the shredded shoulder of his robe, which had borne the brunt of the attack. Beneath the tattered remains of cloth, blood flowed from a deep wound. Strangely, Neame felt no pain. It simply didn't matter. He would be fine, he just had to keep moving. Drawing breath defiantly, he turned towards the city and staggered on.

Barely had he taken a dozen steps when he was hit again, a heavy weight slamming into his head, jerking his body awkwardly and hurling him through the air into a twisted heap.

This time there was no choice but to stay put. His body was broken, his spirit too stunned.

More blood now, from somewhere just above his right eye, clouding his vision with a crimson hue. His head spun.

This was just a bad dream. It couldn't be happening. There was no reason for this to be happening.

And then the Devil looked down upon him, head cocked ever so slightly to one side, deep-set orange eyes glaring hungrily at its prey.

'Lord have mercy,' whispered Brother Neame, as the jaws of death opened wide and moved in for the kill.

ONE

The street wasn't much more than a narrow alley, winding its way behind a row of wooden dwellings, deserted save for a couple of rats foraging through a pile of fetid rubbish.

Suddenly the rats scattered, diving for cover in the secret nooks and crannies that were their city, and the alley was empty.

Or was it? From nothing, a miniature storm sprang into turbulent life, accompanied by a straining, thumping, thunderous echo, and then, tucked away in a discreet corner, a shape slowly took form. Impossibly, out of thin air, a large box topped off with a flashing beacon became solid.

As quickly as it had begun, the wind dropped and the street was silent once more, except for a barely perceptible hum, emanating from the battered blue police box that was now sitting there, as if it were a permanent fixture.

The TARDIS door creaked open, and the Doctor stuck his head out, breathing in enthusiastically.

'Ahh, pre-industrial, unrecycled fresh air. Nothing quite like it.' Wrinkling his nose, the Doctor noticed the stinking heap of rotting vegetables to which the hungry rats were now returning.

'Ew. And this is nothing quite like it.'

The tall, skinny man stepped out into the alley, ruffling his spiky brown hair, and pulled the door closed behind him. 'I'd avoid the salad if I were you, I think it's off,' he advised the rodents. They didn't seem too bothered.

Adjusting the collar of his long coat against the chill evening air, the Doctor paused to get his bearings before amiably wandering off in a random direction.

The medieval city would have been considered little more than a town in twenty-first-century terms, but this was 1139 and, with a population of around two thousand souls, Worcester was a successful and rapidly expanding conurbation.

There was something irresistibly charming about this period in English history, thought the Doctor as he strolled along. Day-to-day life was undeniably hard, the political situation was all over the place, what with the Empress Matilda forcibly attempting to swipe the throne from under King Stephen, and there was a good chance you might be accused of witchcraft at the drop of a hat (pointy or otherwise), but people soldiered on regardless, indomitably, and the Doctor found this heady mix quite thrilling.

There were no high-tech lifestyle solutions here, no celebrity-obsessed mass media, not even those little, bite-sized packets of exotic cheeses that the future held for the descendants of these people. This was the real deal. Life without the custard.

Funny thing, though, there didn't seem to be anyone about.

Every street he walked through had an aura of defensiveness about it, as if the very fabric of each building were colluding with its inhabitants to pretend it wasn't there.

The sky, heavy with thick cloud, had turned from deep grey to dusky blue by the time the Doctor reached the main thoroughfare, and here again all was quiet. Snowflakes began to fall.

In a thousand years or so, this place would be thronging with Christmas shoppers, hurrying from high-street chain to high-street chain, weighed down with gifts destined for online auctions come January. But even here, in the early twelfth century, you'd expect some bustle of activity, some sign of life.

The Doctor liked places that were supposed to be busy to be busy, and if they weren't then there was a good chance that something was up.

Still, if something was up, then he quite liked that too.

There was nothing for it, he'd have to knock on a door and ask what the problem was.

A door slammed somewhere along the street to his left, and in the distance he glimpsed a figure walking hurriedly away from a nearby inn. For a moment he considered trying to catch up with the fast-moving figure, but the inn was much closer, and the warm glow of a fire flickering through its windows offered a more immediate escape from the chilly weather.

The Doctor liked a good inn. Inns were friendly places, always welcoming, full of life, of local colour, and a useful mine of local knowledge for a weary traveller. Maybe he could even get a light snack.

As he approached, he noticed the ground-floor windows were now shuttered securely, blocking out the friendly orange light that had drawn his eyes to the inn in the first place. When he tried the heavy oak door, he found it was bolted. It wasn't closing time, surely? Very odd.

The Doctor shrugged and rapped out what he hoped was a friendly knock on the door.

'Hello, anyone at home?'

No response.

Stepping back, he looked up at the first-floor windows. Was that movement? A pale face, hurriedly darting backwards into the shadows, out of view.

'I don't know which is colder, the weather or the welcome,' he commented to no one in particular.

Not to be deterred, the Doctor knocked again, less

jauntily this time. He didn't plan on stopping until someone took notice.

'Come on,' he muttered, 'it's chillier than the Ood-Sphere out here. Open up.'

'Why won't he give up and leave us in peace?' grumbled John, taking another cautious glance at the annoying figure in the street below.

His wife cowered behind him, clutching a carved wooden candlestick in her hands as if it were a deadly weapon. Wax from the thick white candle rammed into it splattered messily on the floorboards.

'See him off, John. The patrol will be here soon, and we don't want them thinking he's anything to do with us.'

John gave his wife a withering look, which he hoped would disguise his unease. 'You see him off, woman. One look at your grotty old mug and he'll be gone like lightning,' he growled, ducking to avoid the back of her hand as she gave him an angry slap.

'You get down those stairs right now, John Garrud, or so help me I'll brain you with this thing,' she said, wielding the candlestick as proof that she just might.

After a few minutes, the Doctor's persistence was rewarded by the clatter of bolts being thrown back impatiently. The door opened, only a crack, but enough to reveal the red face of a great bear of a man, frowning and unshaven, obviously someone who knew how to handle a troublemaker. Yet the Doctor noted more than a hint of fear in the man's tired eyes, as they furtively scanned the street, making sure this unwelcome stranger was alone.

'We're closed. Go away,' grumbled the man, trying to force the door shut but finding the Doctor's foot blocking its way.

Has to be the landlord, thought the Doctor, wincing. Try flattery and then a brazen lie if need be. That normally does the trick.

'Hello, you must be the proprietor. I'm the Doctor. I've heard great things about this place.' He grinned, grabbing the landlord's hand and shaking it, warmly. 'Been looking forward to popping by for ages. Do you mind if I come in?'

'We're full. Leave us alone.'

'I thought you said you were closed? You can't be closed and full at the same time.'

'Erm, family visiting. Big, big family. All the rooms are taken.' The landlord was flustered, aware that the stranger wasn't going to be given the brush-off. He resorted to pleading. 'Look, please, just go. We don't want any trouble.'

'Honestly, I'm no trouble. Glass of warm milk and straight off to bed, that's me.' The Doctor smiled.

John didn't know what to do. He couldn't let this odd man take his chances out there, could he? Not in good conscience, not with things the way they were.

Then, from further along the street, drifted the sound

of heavy footsteps, armour and chain mail slapping against leather, and John began to panic. The first of the night patrols. The Doctor heard it too, and glanced up the street, curiously. Making up his mind, John grabbed the stranger's collar and dragged him inside, bolting the door firmly shut.

John stared at this 'Doctor' fellow, who'd managed to make himself quite at home already, dumping his overcoat across the back of a tall chair then perching comfortably on the edge of a long table.

'How am I going to explain this to the wife?' thought John.

'Nice decor. Very woody.' The Doctor broke the uncomfortable silence with a disarming grin, looking around the inn's simple interior with interest. A bar and some tables were bathed in the glow of the hearth, where a wood fire crackled and spat. He was just beginning to feel warm again.

A sharp voice cut through the air from the top of the stairs.

'John, is that you? Who are you talking to? Has he gone?'

The staircase creaked as the landlord's wife crept down, still clutching her makeshift weapon. When she caught sight of the Doctor, she froze, glaring several certain deaths at her husband.

John decided to act as if everything was normal. Some hope.

'Gertrude, we have a guest. Can you make up the small room?'

His wife was having none of it. 'No,' she spat. 'I told you to get rid of him.'

'Gert, please. We can't send him back out there. It's too dangerous. The patrols are afoot. He'll only get himself arrested, or worse...'

'Not our problem, John. You don't let a stranger in the house. What if...' She caught the Doctor's eye and looked away, ashamed.

'What if... what?' asked the Doctor. These people weren't being unfriendly, they were genuinely terrified.

'Look, I don't want to cause any trouble. I'll just get my coat and I'll be on my way.' The Doctor hopped off the table and reached for his coat, missing nothing of the quick, silent exchange taking place between the married couple while his back was turned.

Gertrude threw a look of thunder in John's direction, nodding from the Doctor to the door. She wanted him out. Now.

John scowled back and crossed his arms defiantly. 'There'll be no need for that, sir. We'd be happy to accommodate you. Gertrude, the room.' Whatever the danger, he was not going to be responsible for any harm that might otherwise befall this man, whoever he was.

And anyway, they hadn't taken in a paying customer for months, and needed the money. It wasn't as if he had anywhere else to go, so they could pretty much charge him what they wanted.

'Splendid.' The Doctor was pleased. Perhaps now he'd have a chance to ask a few questions. 'Any chance of a bite to eat? I'm famished.'

Gertrude fired a few more imaginary daggers at her husband, and stormed back upstairs.

Outside, the snow was now falling heavily, and a strong wind whipped it past the window.

The Doctor, mopping up the remnants of stew with a chunk of crusty bread, shivered and was rather glad the landlord hadn't turned him out, as his wife had demanded.

Wandering over, carrying two flagons of ale, John Garrud groaned with the strain of middle age, as he lowered his bulky frame onto a stool opposite the Doctor.

'On the house, sir, by way of an apology, for earlier. The missus...' John rolled his eyes, shrugging. 'You know how it is.'

The Doctor eyed his host carefully. 'And quite understandable, what with all this business going on.'

'Mm. Terrible business. These are dark times we're living in. Hard to trust even your regulars, let alone a stranger, such as yourself. No offence,' John stressed. 'Not that I trust some of my regulars at the best of times.'

'None taken,' replied the Doctor.

'If you don't mind me asking, sir, what were you doing out on the streets past the curfew?' the landlord asked, tentatively. 'It's not exactly been good for business, but we've gone a week now without a disappearance, so it must be working.'

A curfew. That at least explained the lack of people out and about, thought the Doctor. But what was it that had this city hiding itself away as soon as night fell?

'Well I'd heard rumours, obviously. That's why I didn't want to risk travelling at night,' the Doctor said, leaning forward, conspiratorially, hoping to coax more from his host.

'Very wise, sir. Who knows when the Huntsman will strike again,' replied John, and the big man shuddered, glancing almost without thinking at the window, as if this Huntsman were hovering right outside, ready to strike.

The Doctor thought for a moment, wracking his brain trying to remember the local legends of this period, the kinds of scare stories parents would tell their children in hushed tones, the implied threat that if they didn't behave then some hideous beastie would creep up and get them...

'Of course. The Devil's Huntsman,' he exclaimed, pleased with himself. 'That's the one with the hellhounds, isn't it? Hunting down lost souls in the Clent Hills, and condemning them to eternal damnation. I love those old ghost stories. What was his name again?'

'Harry Cannab,' John told him, deadly serious. 'And it's no story, Doctor. He's come back. And if Harry Cannab has set his will on hunting your soul, then your fate is sealed, sure as day turns into night.'

'Still, Worcester is a long way from Clent, isn't it? More than a day's ride,' pondered the Doctor. 'Why would he bother travelling all this way south? Aren't there enough souls back home to keep him busy?'

John took a long swig of his ale, and stared glumly at the table top. 'It's a question we've all been pondering, Doctor. All I know is people have gone, disappeared without a trace.' He sniffed. 'Even lost one of my regulars, I have.'

'How long has this been going on?' asked the Doctor, all hint of joviality forgotten.

John had another drink. If there was one thing to lift the spirits of a good innkeeper, it was spreading local gossip to his customers.

'Been nigh on three months, since that monk fella didn't turn up when he was supposed to. Caused a right stink up at the Cathedral, it did. Then we started to hear about them as had gone missing in the villages hereabouts. We thought we'd be safe in the city, but then people started talking about the Huntsman...' John paused, and the silence was deafening. 'I suppose it was only a matter of time before he struck again. Not three streets from here. Robert Marsh, his name was. Didn't know him, but they said he deserved better. When they found him, down Sidbury way, his body was turned inside out.'

They sat quietly for a few minutes, lost in their individual thoughts.

Whatever it was out there, it was no phantasmagorical legend, the Doctor knew that much.

At the heart of every myth there lay some grain of truth, some real event that had had a profound impact on those involved. He should know, having played a part in creating a few himself. He was the Oncoming Storm after all. Even his own race had passed into legend. Tales of mythical monsters somehow became more 'real' as each generation passed the story on to the next. Something that happened to a friend of a friend, who'd heard it from someone, who'd heard it some place else, until the myth gained a life of its own. But rarely did the original actually turn up in person, centuries later.

Ignoring himself, of course.

No, outside there was a blood and bone creature, stalking this city and the surrounding countryside. It was probably nothing more than a wild animal, but it was as real as it was deadly.

A few hours had passed since their talk, and John had long since drifted off to sleep, snoring gently.

The Doctor stood by the shuttered window, listening intently to the quiet stillness of the night, all sound deadened by the thick snowfall. His thoughts turned to the families huddled inside their homes, no doubt fearing this would be the night the Huntsman's wrath would fall upon them. The Doctor wondered how many sleepless nights his host had spent sitting down here, sword at the ready, fighting fatigue to protect his wife.

The scream of some kind of bird rang out in the night sky, and John was awake, scrambling to his feet.

'Doctor. Did you hear that?' he whispered, hoarsely, eyes wide.

Then the strangled howl came again. No, it was different this time, a human scream, and both men tensed, ears straining.

Gertrude clattered down the stairs, dropping her candlestick, and threw herself into her husband's arms, gripping him tightly.

'John. It's him. It's the Huntsman. He's back,' she sobbed, shaking.

The Doctor threw on his coat and made for the door.

'Don't go out there. It's not safe,' cried John, but it was too late. The Doctor was already haring off towards the horrible screeching.

'Leave him, John. If the Huntsman gets him, that's his lookout. At least he isn't coming for us.' She slammed the door shut and had it bolted in one swift movement.

The terrible screaming had stopped. Skidding to a halt, the Doctor listened keenly for a moment, trying to work out where in this maze of narrow streets it had emanated from. Making the best guess he could, he ran on, knowing it was now almost certainly too late.

His fears were confirmed as he hurtled around a corner and into a small yard. There was a body, or at least bits of one, scattered across the yard. Crouching over it, a dark, inhuman figure tore at the remains with dirty, yellow, bloodied teeth.

It stopped. Distracted from its feast, and becoming

aware of the Doctor's presence, the beast stretched its thin, muscular legs, unfurling wide, translucent wings, and turned to face the newcomer. Orange eyes locked on the Doctor's, and it screamed, a deafening, bloodcurdling, venomous howl.

This was no mythical beast, no local bogeyman. This was a creature of which to be truly fearful.

'Krillitane,' whispered the Doctor.

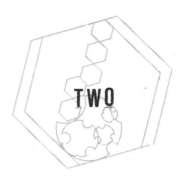

TWO

Emily pulled back the hood of her all-weather jacket, and ran her fingers through her short blonde hair. With a sigh, she raised her binocs, scanning the rooftops for any hint of movement. Still there was no sign of her prey.

Where the hell were they? It was cold, she was tired, and yet again she'd been unable to get the confirmation her client needed.

It had taken a week to position the Bio-locator Pods at strategic points across the city. They were low-energy units, impossible to detect with security scanners, and she'd optimistically hoped they would give results first time out. Instead she hadn't picked up so much as a blip for the past three nights.

Stuffing the binocs back into her satchel, Emily

decided to call it a night. The snowstorm was making it all but impossible to see anything anyway, even from this hillside vantage point, high in an aged oak tree overlooking the city.

She'd taken a risk, staying out here in the open, knowing how dangerous it was, but she had a job to do and as soon as she'd done it she could get off this backwards rock and put the whole sorry business behind her.

A sudden flare caught her eye as it skittered across the screen on her scanning unit, catching Emily by surprise. She grabbed the device and checked its readings. There – an electromagnetic power surge in the city below, as unlikely as ice on a star. It had lasted no more than a second. Dammit.

She grimaced. A malfunction in one of the Pods, or perhaps this dratted weather was playing havoc with the signal. Either way, there was nothing for it, she'd have to head into town and check each and every Pod until she found the shot one.

Unhappily, the young woman packed up her gear and clambered resignedly to the ground.

Fifteen checked and fully functional Pods later, Emily's mood hadn't improved. It didn't help that she'd spent most of her time dodging the heavily armed groups of men that were patrolling the streets. They weren't hard to avoid, but it had slowed her progress to a point where she might as well have been crawling.

Checking the coast was clear, she crept out of her most recent hiding place, and headed for the location of Pod Sixteen.

Annoyingly, she found a blue shed was blocking access to the small, spherical bio-detector. The shed definitely hadn't been there when she'd activated the Pod, a few days previously.

'Stupid place to build an outhouse,' Emily muttered, irritated, as she tried to figure out a way to get past the obstacle. The young woman frowned. There was something strange about this box. It didn't feel right, as if it didn't belong. Tentatively, she reached out with her gloved hand, sensing a slight vibration in the atmosphere surrounding the box…

And snatched it back as a horrific scream echoed through the streets. All thoughts of this mysterious structure were instantly wiped from her mind. Perhaps tonight hadn't been such a waste of time after all. Her prey was close at hand.

She was in no rush to get herself killed, and there was no point confronting anyone. All she had to do was get one good image grab, and she could do that without anyone realising she was ever there.

Maybe this box could be of use after all, Emily thought, and quickly scaled its sides, using its recessed panels as footholds and bracing herself between the box and the nearby wall. Once on its roof, she was able to step across to the wooden tiles of the closest building. Good. Much less chance of getting spotted up here.

A few carefully judged leaps later, and Emily had found what she was looking for. Crouching low, she peered over the edge into the open space below. A large, inhuman shape was moving against the bright snow.

Scrabbling for her binocs, Emily thumbed the record button before zooming in and focusing, and immediately regretted her haste.

Filling the viewfinder was a flap of crimson flesh, hanging from the jaws of something hideous. A head that seemed to be all teeth moved into view, and she got a glimpse of a tiny, evil eye. The thing flicked the meat fully into its mouth, blood dripping over its lips, and her stomach turned. Panning away sharply, Emily discovered the source of the creature's meal. A body, lying dead in the snow. Suddenly a blurry figure sped through the frame, and Emily zoomed out, enough to make out the silhouette of a thin man in a very long coat, now standing very still and staring at the creature

It had not, as yet, registered the man's presence, but when it did he would be a dead man. With mounting horror, Emily watched as the creature, a giant muscular beast of taut skin stretched over joint and sinew, lifted its head and turned towards its next victim.

The Doctor froze, and the alien predator took a threatening step towards him, tensing its muscles, ready to pounce. Then it stopped in its tracks. Nostrils flaring, the Krillitane took in the Doctor's scent, and cocked its monstrous head to one side. Was it confused?

Suddenly, with a frustrated, hungry glare at the Doctor, it flexed its powerful wings and took to the air, sweeping up into the night sky and away.

The Doctor exhaled a mighty breath. Sometimes, when tearing along at full pelt, his sense of self-preservation couldn't keep up. Donna had always been telling him to slow down, and he'd never listened. Maybe she'd had a point.

'That was a bit close,' he swallowed.

Only now that both hearts weren't in imminent danger of being torn out through his ribs, did the Doctor become aware of the clatter of approaching boots. The night patrol was coming. It must have been their scent that had rattled the Krillitane, its hunting instincts honed through generations of scavenging and adopting the strengths of other races. Thank heavens for medieval personal hygiene; the creature must've smelt them a mile off. Odd that it hadn't picked up his scent, though.

Odder still, what on Earth was a Krillitane doing in medieval England? They had been humanoid themselves at one point, so there could be little of any interest to them in human DNA, or the planet's current level of technology.

Judging by its appearance, it must have been one of the first generations to have adopted the wings of the Bessan. The neck was longer than the last time he'd encountered them, some 800 years in Earth's future, and the tail much longer, with a forked tip. Very much the traditional representation of the Devil in this period. How apt.

Then an unwelcome thought struck the Doctor, followed by a sinking feeling. Here he was, alone, with a rather brutally murdered body lying at his feet. To the casual observer, this probably wouldn't look good. To the patrol, already on the hunt for a killer and very close now, this would look very, very bad indeed...

Then something caught his eye, a glint of metal, partially buried in the snow and just beyond the grasp of the messy corpse.

'Hello, looks like you dropped something. Don't suppose you'll have much use for it now.' He reached out, gingerly picking up the blood-spattered object. It wasn't much larger than a palm-sized computer or a mobile phone, a thumb pad and big red button filling the lower half of its battered fascia, while its small screen had been rendered cracked and useless, punctured by the fearsome claw of the Krillitane.

Whatever the device's purpose, it wasn't of Earth origin, and that suggested that this poor chap, to whom it almost certainly belonged, wasn't of Earth origin either. Curiouser and curiouser.

Scuffling footsteps now almost on top of him, the Doctor pocketed the ruined device and spun round, just as half a dozen or so soldiers burst into the yard, raising their pikes and swords defensively.

'It was him,' the Doctor gushed, breathlessly, as if he had only just arrived on the scene himself. 'It was the Huntsman, I saw him. He flew off.' He pointed upwards, in no specific direction. 'That way.'

The soldiers looked at each other, uncertainty clouding their faces, their pikes wavering as they took in the dreadful scene before them. A burly man with a scar above his left eye, whom the Doctor assumed to be their leader, wasn't in any doubt about what had happened here.

'I want him bound and gagged *now*,' he barked. 'Get to it.' He turned to his messenger, a terrified-looking young lad who couldn't tear his eyes from the Doctor. 'Get to the Castle as fast as you can. Report the capture and return with reinforcements. Go.'

'Hang on. I had nothing to do with this,' protested the Doctor, as the soldiers closed in around him. 'Look, not a spec of… well, him on me. I'd have hardly had time to nip off to the dry cleaners now, would I? Just give me a chance to exfflemffle…'

A gag being forced into the Doctor's mouth muffled his objections and, as the soldiers grabbed his arms and roughly tied his hands behind his back, he decided it was probably not the best time to put up a fight. These men were on edge, and carrying a serious armoury of very sharp weapons. Not a good combination. At some point he was bound to be taken before someone in a position of authority, someone he could reason with. He'd talk his way out of this tricky situation then.

As his troops continued their work, Captain Darke stared coldly at the prisoner, careful to keep his distance, taking the measure of this man, this supposed demon that had terrorised the city.

Darke was a career soldier, and had fought in truly bloody battles on home soil and abroad, even as far away as the Holy Lands, yet nothing compared to the carnage before him now. What kind of beast could do this? Was it even possible that this could have been the work of a man?

With the prisoner secured, Darke walked quietly, deliberately towards him, and spoke in little more than a harsh whisper. These words were for the Doctor's ears alone.

'I'm a soldier, have been since I was a boy. I've seen death. I've seen the horrors that one man can unleash upon another, and I long ago abandoned superstition. I know that darkness lies in the heart of men, and you…' he paused, disgusted. 'You, my friend, have the eyes of a killer.'

The Doctor could only stare back, widening his eyes in a silent protest of innocence, but it was to no avail. Darke turned away, raising his voice so all could hear.

'We have him. We have the Huntsman,' he cried.

Was that him, Emily wondered? The target she'd been searching for? Those clothes definitely weren't local, she reasoned, sizing up the tall, smartly dressed man. If it was him, then he looked nothing like she'd imagined from the scant details in his biog.

Pulling up the binocs' main menu, she selected a couple of clear images and saved the grabs to its data drive. She could run an ID analysis sweep back at base later but, with that creature on the loose, she was anxious to get indoors.

The scene unfolding below didn't look good, however. If that was the man she was hunting, then it would do her no favours if the natives executed him. They had arrived on the scene too late to witness the alien creature's escape, and had obviously assumed this rather less fearsome catch was the culprit. If only they knew.

As she watched, the patrol began to move off, two soldiers ahead of the prisoner, with four bringing up the rear. One solitary guard had been left to watch over the bloody remains, and she didn't envy his task.

The check on the Pods would have to wait, she decided, and she set off in pursuit of the prisoner and escort.

As the small group marched through the narrow streets and alleys, the Doctor became aware of a growing hubbub rising in their wake. Word was spreading, and the people wanted a glimpse of the Devil's Huntsman.

Shutters were swinging open, people spilling out onto the streets through previously bolted doors. Gatherings of curious onlookers quickly grew into a crowd, at first merely following at a distance, but soon surrounding the troupe, increasing in size until it began to achieve critical mass, pressing in angrily upon the six soldiers and their prisoner.

The atmosphere was sparking with heightened emotion, and the Doctor sensed the mood was turning ugly. The people of Worcester had lived under the yolk of fear for months and, as far as they were concerned, here was the cause of their misery, a target upon whom they were ready to exact vengeance. Who could blame them, thought the Doctor. Just a shame they had the wrong alien.

This trip had been on a downward slope since he'd stumbled upon that Krillitane. OK, so it hadn't eaten him, which was undeniably a good thing, but maybe this time he'd run out of lucky breaks.

'They're going to kill him,' hissed Emily, through gritted teeth. It was no good. She'd have to risk direct intervention, and worry about the consequences later. There were a few cover stories she could call on if need be, but she had to move, and move fast.

Stripping off her jacket, revealing a close enough approximation of local costume underneath, Emily stowed her kit deep in the roof's eaves. They would be safe enough from prying eyes there until she had a chance to retrieve them.

'Here goes.'

'Keep back,' shouted Darke, pushing back another surge of citizens, some shouting abuse at the bound and gagged prisoner. This was getting nasty, thought Darke, as he bellowed an urgent order to his men: 'Close ranks and present arms.'

The troops drew their weapons and moved closer to the Doctor, facing down the increasingly angry mob.

The Doctor became vaguely aware of a young woman, fighting her way through the crowd nearby, crying out for her husband. He hoped nothing too bad had befallen her partner, but there were rather more pressing matters demanding his attention, like that noose he'd noticed being swung over a gibbet, a short distance away.

Suddenly, the same woman had forced her way past the armed guards.

'Husband. What have they done to you?' she exclaimed, rather theatrically.

The Doctor was more than a little taken aback when she tore the gag from his mouth, threw her arms around his neck and kissed him, passionately and repeatedly. Even if she'd given him the chance, he was too shocked to respond.

'Oh, my love.' The girl turned her head to the Captain. 'Untie him, you beastly men. This is my husband.'

'Get away from the prisoner.' Darke attempted to drag the hysterical woman away, but she struggled and kicked so hard that he had to step back.

A horn sounded, and the mob fell silent and backed away as a full squad of soldiers rushed into the fray. Darke breathed a sigh of relief. In the confusion, he'd almost forgotten he'd sent the messenger for back-up. The lad would earn a commendation for carrying out his orders so swiftly.

An uneasy quiet had fallen on the crowd, the wind of retribution taken from their sails. Darke took advantage of the sudden calm.

'Return to your homes,' his grizzled voice boomed. 'This city remains under curfew, and those caught flouting it will be flogged.'

Mumbling and muttering, the crowd began to disperse, hurried along by the additional troops whose arrival could not have been more welcome.

Only this crazed woman remained, clinging on to her so-called husband like a limpet.

'Release him at once,' Emily demanded again. 'You've got the wrong man.'

'That's what I've been trying to tell them,' piped up the Doctor. 'Dearest wife,' he added for good measure, grateful at the unexpected appearance of this young blonde woman, whoever she was.

'Guards, restrain her,' ordered Darke. This was the last thing he needed.

'Unhand my wife, sir,' bluffed the Doctor, an indignant tone in his voice. If this soldier could be persuaded they were married, he was happy to play along, at least for the time being. 'I had nothing to do with that murder. My wife heard a scream, and I rushed out to help. I could have ended up being the Huntsman's dinner.'

'We live nearby,' interjected the girl, helpfully. 'If you hadn't arrived, sir, the Huntsman would have surely devoured my husband. I am forever in your debt.' She moved away from the Doctor and hugged Darke, gratefully.

Darke extricated himself from her embrace, and looked from one to the other. They made an odd pair, their clothing too well made for them to be of peasant stock. If they had connections, then to cross them would not be wise. Perhaps he had misjudged the situation, in the heat of the moment? Darke had to admit that, at best, the evidence he had against this man was circumstantial. Still, there was definitely something about the prisoner of which to be wary. He had something of the Devil about him, and Darke wasn't going to just let him wander off unguarded.

'Release him,' the soldier ordered, finally, and one of his men cut the Doctor's bonds.

'Thank you,' said the Doctor, rubbing at the sore rope burns on his wrists. 'I'm Smith, John Smith, and this is my wife… Mrs Smith.'

'Save your thanks. You will be confined to your dwelling until your story can be corroborated.'

The woman was now hugging the prisoner again, face buried in his chest, but the intimacy seemed forced to the Captain.

Darke nodded at two of his troops. 'Take them to their lodgings and make sure they're secure. I'll return at daybreak to take a statement.'

As the guards ushered them away, the Doctor stole a quick glance at the girl who'd saved his life, and noted her breeches and boots were both made from artificial fibre. Yet another visitor to planet Earth, then? This place was getting more like an intergalactic bus station by the minute.

THREE

Elation and blind panic fuelled the flight of the Krillitane they called Toeclaw, as she forced her wings ever harder, desperate to put distance between herself and the city.

It wouldn't be long before they realised what had happened, and she knew it was only a matter of time before they pushed the button that would end her life. She had to get out of range.

The man-thing had deserved his death, and Toeclaw had enjoyed killing him, her belly still warm with meat and the thrill of the hunt.

Muscles straining, weakened and unfit through lack of use, she felt her strength failing. If she could only keep her wings beating until she reached the hills to the south of the city and could lose herself in their rocky outcrops and valleys, the power of the signal might be dampened sufficiently and she would be safe.

No sooner had this thought, this hope, crossed her mind than a flash of indescribable pain burst across her shoulders. Her wings folded and crumpled, useless and heavy, and she was falling, tumbling, towards the ground. Her body became numb, as the muscular spasms that engulfed her body began to subside, and she felt consciousness slipping away.

She would die on her own terms, not theirs, she resolved. Not like this.

With a start, the Krillitane regained consciousness. She was lying in the dark shadows of a woodland copse and, as far as she could tell from a quick examination, she didn't appear to have damaged herself too badly. The trees had evidently cushioned her fall. Toeclaw closed her wings tightly around her body, shivering with cold and pain. This would serve as a safe enough hiding place for the remainder of the night.

Then another sudden, agonising jolt of energy shot through her spine, a reminder of the accursed inhibitor, buried deep in the muscle tissue at the nape of her neck. It hadn't killed her, but it would have to be removed.

Twisting awkwardly to reach past her wings, Toeclaw probed at her skin with clawed fingers, tracing the contours of the rough scar where the insidious device had been surgically implanted. She could feel an uneven lump, slightly to the left of her spine, and imagined its wiry tendrils hooked into her central nervous system, like a web of steel barbs.

Toeclaw gathered her last reserves of energy. She knew there was a risk of permanent damage, and a high likelihood that the device had been booby-trapped, but she would not be free until the offensive object had been disposed of. Digging a single claw into the peak of the scar, she made an incision, slicing slowly downwards, deep into her flesh. Gritting her fangs against the pain, she forced two fingers into the open wound until they located the metal and plastic object, closer to the surface of the skin than she'd expected. Perhaps it had been dislodged or damaged in her fall? Either way, she was filled with a new confidence that its removal would not be as life-threatening as she'd feared. Gripping the device's smooth sides as tightly as she could, she yanked, hard and, with a roar of triumph, tore the inhibitor from her body and threw it aside, as far as she could.

Toeclaw blinked and glanced at the object lying in the snow a few metres away, with contempt. She was pleased to be free of it at last.

This was not over. As soon as she had regained her strength, she would return to release her brothers and sisters from bondage, and then the feast would truly begin.

Captain Darke glanced uneasily at the sky as the rough-hewn wooden coffin was loaded onto a cart, beginning its short journey to the Castle.

He'd taken his time examining the corpse, and had now satisfied himself that the man they'd captured could not have been responsible. The severity of the attack had been too voracious to have come from human hands. While glad that they finally had an eye witness who might provide the answers to many questions, the fact remained that there was still a killer at large.

'Sir. Orders from the Sheriff.' A messenger had arrived, and he handed Darke a folded and sealed slip of parchment.

'What was his mood?' he asked the patiently waiting soldier. It was a common talking point amongst the troops that the new Sheriff could be somewhat volatile and, despite his rank, Darke was still considered very much one of the men.

'Quieter than usual, sir, if that's possible.'

'Never a good sign,' muttered the Captain, tearing open the message.

As he'd suspected, further investigation would have to wait until morning. He was to make his report on the night's events immediately, and he wasn't looking forward to it.

Making his way to the Castle, Darke paid little attention to the additional fortifications and manpower installed by the Sheriff when he had taken up his post a few months earlier. Worcester held a strategic importance, and the ongoing political situation had worsened with news that Matilda and her supporters were now in England.

Even so, Darke couldn't help but think that the bolstered defences were overkill. The Sheriff struck him as a man governed by paranoia, and that was not a positive trait for someone with so much responsibility.

Aides ushered Darke into the Sheriff's chamber, and he waited patiently as his superior busied himself behind an ornate desk.

The Sheriff was a small man with a neatly clipped beard and shaven head. Intense, obsessive and a little bit precious. A true politician, thought Darke. Their relationship had never been anything other than uncomfortable.

'Welcome, Captain. I hear you allowed the Huntsman to have his fun and games again this evening.' The Sheriff continued to read through documents as he said this, as if Darke's presence were an inconvenience.

'We almost had him, sir, but he was disturbed by a citizen and fled before we could make an arrest.'

'A citizen breaking my curfew.' Looking up, finally, the Sheriff's eyes were hard and unfriendly. 'I trust you had him suitably punished?' he said icily.

Darke continued undeterred. 'He is the only witness to have seen the Huntsman and lived, my Lord. I thought it best to take him into custody…'

'Ah yes, thereby causing a riot in the streets as the people tried to lynch him. Tell me, Captain Darke, are you aware of the concept of subtlety?'

'The situation escalated, sir, yes. Word spread. I don't know how, but there was no way I could have predicted that. The crowd was brought under control and dispersed, and we now have the witness held under supervision at his dwelling.'

The Sheriff stood and walked over to a shuttered window, peering at the world outside through a tiny hole in a twisted knot in the wood. He remained there, in silent contemplation.

'If he hadn't broken the curfew,' Darke continued, 'come morning we would be looking for yet another missing person, without any clue as to what happened.'

Still no response.

'Had I not been called here to report on events of which you seem quite clearly aware, then perhaps by now he would have given us some answers.'

Darke had risen to the bait despite himself, and the Sheriff turned his cold gaze upon the Captain. His lips twitched into a brief, mirthless smile, as if raising Darke's hackles had pleased him.

'Have you identified the body?' he asked.

'No, sir. It was too badly disfigured.' Darke recovered his composure. 'As yet we've not had any reports of missing citizens, so it's possible he may have been a visitor to the city.'

'An outsider?' the Sheriff hissed.

'It's possible, yes but…'

'I want the patrols doubled, and lookouts posted beyond the city walls. Henceforth no one enters or leaves this city without my express permission, until further notice.'

'But my Lord…' Darke had seen firsthand the strength of feeling amongst the people. These new restrictions would only serve to foster further unrest.

'For all we know, the Huntsman is an agent of our enemies, sent to undo our resolve and break our will,' continued the Sheriff. 'Bring me your prisoner. I would question him myself.'

The Doctor sat back down on the chair he'd vacated a few minutes earlier, crossing his arms with a huff. A brief search of the room had turned up nothing more than the simple trappings of medieval life and some lint. Not so much as an extraterrestrial sausage to give him a clue as to his host's reasons for being on Earth.

The room was basic and sparsely furnished, but comfortable enough, and the Doctor was glad of the cosy calm it afforded, after the previous hour's tension.

He'd been pleasantly surprised when the girl had led them to these rented rooms, on the second floor of a well-appointed house in the north of the city, as he'd half-suspected she didn't have anywhere to take them at all.

The soldiers who had accompanied them were now stationed in the street below, having made a cursory inspection of the property when they'd arrived, so for now the Doctor had a quiet moment alone to think.

Behind the closed door of the other room, his new 'wife' busied herself in what was, presumably, her bedchamber.

'So, how was it for you?' asked the Doctor, loudly enough to get her attention. After a moment the door creaked open and Emily stuck her head out.

'I'm sorry, how was what?' she asked, frowning.

'The big day. I mean, it's the biggest day of your life, isn't it, your wedding day. All those arrangements.' He toyed with an apple he'd helped himself to from a bowl on the table. 'All those in-laws meeting for the first time. That embarrassing uncle dancing just a bit too closely to the bridesmaid....' The Doctor took a big bite of his apple, and raised a questioning eyebrow. 'Shame I missed it.'

The young woman looked sheepish and stepped into the room. 'It was the best I could think of. Sorry. They were going to hang you, you know.'

'I know. Not most people's first choice of activity for a honeymoon. So, thanks and all that, but who exactly are you?'

She shrugged. 'Just a local girl. Nothing special about me.'

Had he not already stumbled across two alien visitors that night, the Doctor might have believed her. As it was, her being there was too much of a coincidence.

'No, no, no, no, no. You're about as local as I am, and I'm a long way from home. Otherwise you'd have been helping them with the rope.' The Doctor waited for a reply. 'Fine, I'll go first then. I'm the Doctor, pleased to meet you. Your turn.'

'My name is Emily Parr,' she replied, indignantly, 'as

if you didn't know that already. I suppose my father sent you after me? Well you can tell him he can send as many bounty hunters as he likes, I'm not going back.'

There was a hint of duplicity in her blue eyes, and the Doctor wasn't sure she was being entirely truthful.

'Bounty…? Emily, I'm not a bounty hunter, and I've no idea who your dad is. I was just passing through and fancied a breath of fresh air, that's all,' he reassured her.

'And you just happened to turn up here, about a billion light years from the nearest transit station?' Emily asked, sarcastically.

'I come here quite a lot, actually. It's a nice planet.' The Doctor felt obligated to defend the honour of Earth; it was like a second home to him. He realised with irritation that the girl had put him on the back foot. 'Hold on, I was the one asking the questions.'

'Well you can't expect me not to have a few of my own. It took me a long time to find a planet this far off the trade routes, where I could make a new life for myself, and then you turn up out of nowhere. What am I supposed to think?'

The Doctor really wasn't prepared to argue the point. 'I'm sorry if you've got family troubles, really I am, but this isn't the safest planet to hide on right now. If you can, you should leave, and as soon as possible.'

'Nice try, mister, but I'm not going anywhere. You'd have a trace on me the moment I broke orbit.' Emily crossed her arms, and gave the Doctor a defiant glare.

'Oh, for the mists of Clom,' groaned the Doctor. 'I have

nothing to do with your family. For whatever reason, you saved my life earlier, and I'm just trying to return the favour. Honestly. You'll be in terrible danger if you stay here.'

'From the local wildlife, you mean?' Emily shuddered. Fear of that animal was one thing she didn't need to lie about. 'It's got the locals so rattled, I've had a hard time blending in.'

'It's called a Krillitane, and it's not exactly a native.' The Doctor looked at the young woman. Her cover story was pretty tenuous, and he felt certain she knew more than she was letting on. Perhaps a little nudge might get some truth out of her.

Digging into his capacious pockets, the Doctor retrieved the device he'd found earlier, turning it over in his hand.

'What do you make of this?' he asked and threw it to Emily, who caught the silver white object adeptly. The Doctor watched her, carefully.

'I don't know,' she said with a noncommittal shrug. 'Could be some kind of tracking monitor, or a geo-location node. It's broken, though.'

'Yeah, I'd figured that much out for myself, thanks. Problem is, that's alien tech, and it belonged to the man that the Krillitane murdered.'

'So he was an off-worlder?' Emily thought aloud, as she studied the device.

Now this was unexpected. She wasn't familiar with these Krillitane creatures, but she knew that this one was being used to hunt humans, for reasons she couldn't begin to imagine. She'd assumed the victim had been just another hapless Earthling, but perhaps the beast had turned on its master? Perhaps the Doctor wasn't the man she'd suspected him to be after all and really was a random traveller, as he claimed. Or perhaps he was unwanted competition? This job had seemed so simple when she'd taken it on.

'Have you noticed anything out of the ordinary since you arrived? I mean, apart from the string of brutal murders and a very tall winged killing machine?' asked the Doctor.

Emily threw the device back to him, shaking her head. 'Nothing. I've been keeping my head down, trying not to draw attention to myself. I just figured that's how life is here.'

'Don't underestimate the people of this little planet,' the Doctor enthused. 'Once they invent the digital watch there'll be no stopping them. In just eight hundred years they'll have set foot on their moon. In celestial terms, that's a spit in the sawdust. A hundred years after that and they'll have colonised the planet next door...' The Doctor caught himself, noticing Emily's expression of disbelief. 'Probably,' he added. 'Anyway...'

He leapt from his chair, and paced across the room, deep in thought.

'I need to find out what the Krillitanes are up to and, more importantly, where they're hiding. You've been lucky, so far. Krillitanes don't often travel alone. Where there's one, there's a dozen more, and they don't take kindly to people interfering with their plans.'

'You mean they're intelligent?' Emily frowned.

'Oh yeah. They're brilliant. Stupidly brilliant. Last time I met them they'd manipulated the intelligence of human children, turning them into an organic network of computers to crack the Skasas Paradigm and conquer all of time and space.'

'The… what?'

'The universal theory that would have seen the Krillitanes become more powerful than their own gods. As I say, brilliant, but they do suffer from delusions of grandeur. Luckily, I turned up with my pet dog and we stopped them.' The Doctor smiled, remembering the friends who'd fought alongside him. Good times.

'Their whole plan revolved around the use of high technology and fertile, well-educated young minds, which won't be on offer here for centuries.' The Doctor paused for thought. 'Well, we can worry about what they're up to later. First we've got to figure out where they've set up shop.'

'It has to be somewhere out of town,' she suggested. 'Creatures like that couldn't stay hidden.'

'Didn't I mention? They're shape-shifters. Well, morphic illusionists to be precise… They'll have adopted human form, blended in. I could be one. You could be one.'

'Well I'm not,' protested Emily.

'Neither am I,' replied the Doctor quickly. There was

a moment's uncomfortable silence, as they eyed each other up suspiciously, before the Doctor spoke again.

'Right then. Neither of us is about to flap our wings and make an early breakfast of the other. That's a good thing. So... we're looking for a location within the city walls, big enough to accommodate a large group of humans without anyone paying any attention...'

'Oh my God,' Emily gasped with a sudden realisation. 'The Sheriff.'

It was all so obvious. Why hadn't she given more credence to the tittle-tattle of shopkeepers and street hawkers? Too involved in her mission, and too much of an amateur to recognise the importance of background detail, that was why.

'The old Sheriff must have been one of the first victims of the Krillitane.' Emily spoke quickly, struggling to remember what she'd heard. 'When the new Sheriff took up residence, he arrived with a small garrison of his own troops, and immediately put the night curfew in place.'

'Brilliant.' The Doctor's eyes sparkled. 'Perfect cover by day, and free reign of the city by night. And the Sheriff's job comes with its own Castle. What else could a covert alien taskforce ask for?'

The Doctor grabbed his coat and headed for the door. 'Well, come on then.'

'What?' Emily was nonplussed.

The Doctor grinned. 'Let's go and have a look.'

FOUR

'What do you mean, "he had a parchment"?' Darke could not believe what he was hearing. Some kind of house arrest when the guards simply let the prisoner wander off.

Butcher rubbed his eyes, trying to clear the muddy confusion that had filled his head since his recent encounter with the prisoner. 'In a small leather pouch, sir. A parchment, upon which it was written that John Smith is on official business for King Stephen himself, and that he should be allowed the freedom of the city. He said I'd get a promotion, or the Victoria Cross at the very least. Or something called a Blue Peter Badge?'

Darke glared at Butcher. 'And you read this parchment yourself, did you? Having acquired the learning to do so some time between evensong and midnight?'

'Well, he told us what it said, sir,' Butcher admitted miserably.

'So you let him go.' Darke grimaced. If the Sheriff got wind of this, who knew what would happen. He wasn't known for being particularly forgiving. Looking at the forlorn foot soldier before him, the Captain was hardly surprised. His men were way beyond breaking point, and it was a wonder they weren't making more mistakes. 'How long ago did they leave?'

Hewse, the soldier who'd been watching the back door, piped up, hoping to mitigate whatever punishment Butcher had earned them. 'Not very long at all, sir. Minutes at most. They can't have gone far. We'd have heard the alarm by now, if they'd got as far as the city wall.'

Butcher continued to squirm. 'It must have been witchcraft, Captain. That Smith fellow used magic on me, or something.'

'Magic? Yes, I'm sure that's what it was. Not that you're a gullible old fool a child could have tricked his way past. Get back to the barracks, both of you. And don't mention this to anybody. I shall deal with the matter myself.' The Captain watched his troops march sullenly away. Nothing that had happened tonight made any sense, and questions were beginning to pile upon questions.

Tonight's attack had had a different feel about it. The Huntsman hadn't struck within the city walls since the curfew had been introduced, and previous victims had been snatched and taken to a more remote spot before being eviscerated, rather than devoured in such a public place. Darke knew it was unusual for a predator to change its hunting patterns to such a degree, and this was surely true for mystical hunters as much as for animals. So something had changed.

Now this John Smith, if that was his real name, had disappeared along with his female friend. Was she really his wife, or merely an accomplice? Darke couldn't decide, but it seemed obvious that they were here for a reason. Perhaps this enigmatic visitor really was on a mission for the King? He was certain something bigger was happening here than mere superstition could account for, and he was determined to get to the bottom of it.

The fugitives must have left some evidence in the house, Darke reasoned, and made his way up the stairs to the main room. It didn't take long to ascertain that there was nothing of any interest in there, not even personal effects. He tried the door to the bedchamber. It was locked.

He was in no mood for an obstruction as minor as a missing key, and kicked the door hard with a well-aimed boot. It crashed open, banging against the interior wall, and Darke stormed into the small room. Moonlight reflecting off the snow outside cast a square of blue light against the far wall, allowing him to make out the shape of an unmade bed, a chamber pot tucked underneath it, and a chair that had seen better days. The only storage in the room was a medium-sized crate under the window. Rushing over to examine it, Darke barely registered a floorboard creak and sag under his weight.

Wrenching the crate open, Darke was immediately disappointed to find nothing more than a small collection of blankets and threadbare garments inside. The crate was otherwise empty. The Captain smashed his fist on the window frame in frustration. If this had been a marital home, then the loving couple must have been very happy together indeed, having no need for the kind of trinkets and keepsakes that defined most relationships. Darke was in no doubt now that the Smiths were nothing of the sort.

Poor old Hewse had been right about one thing – if they had headed for the city walls, the alarm would certainly have been raised. This meant they had another objective. Where would they have gone? Staring into the night through the room's small window for inspiration, Darke's searching gaze drifted towards the Cathedral tower. He'd decided, years ago, that the good Lord would not provide him with any of the answers he sought, and he saw no reason why this would change now. On the other side of the Cathedral grounds were the Castle and the bed he hadn't had a full night's sleep in for weeks. Tonight was looking like no exception.

In his reverie, he almost missed a black shape on a rooftop, not more than three streets away, until it moved against the snow, reaching for something hidden in the building's eaves. Tensing, Darke peered at the shape, trying to make sense of it. He couldn't be sure, but it looked like Smith's partner. If he moved quickly, there was a chance he might catch them.

The Captain made for the door, but stopped, this time more aware of that creaking floorboard. He realised he'd been an idiot. The crate had been placed in plain view, an obvious distraction from the real hiding place. Darke brought his heal down hard and, with a sudden crack of splintering wood, his foot smashed straight through the floor. He snatched at the remains of the floorboard, which had split and evaporated under his boot, throwing them to one side impatiently, and allowed himself a grim smile. He'd found what he'd been searching for.

Hidden under the boards was a collection of objects the like of which he had never seen – silver and white canisters of metal, the size of apples; pouches made of some transparent material that had the feel of polished leather; brightly coloured gourds containing who knew what – and none of them he could identify as having any practical use. Except for…

Darke reached in and carefully took hold of a pipe, the length of a man's leg and as black as coal. It had a dark, not quite wooden stock at one end, and a grip crafted from the same cold, hard material halfway along its shaft. On its top side was a complicated eyeglass, and underneath was a single lever that would accommodate the squeeze of a finger. He could feel the object's power, sense its deadly purpose, and, though the concept of a rifle was centuries beyond his comprehension, he knew instinctively that this was a weapon.

***

'Haven't you finished up there yet?' whispered the Doctor, urgently. Emily had been quite insistent on retrieving some stuff she'd hidden earlier, and she was taking her time about it. The Doctor wasn't keen on remaining out in the open any longer than they had to, and glanced around nervously. A tap on the shoulder caused both his hearts to skip a beat.

'Yep, just about,' whispered Emily with a cheeky grin, having crept silently up behind him. She adjusted her backpack and got her bearings. 'Come on. The Castle's this way. We can cut across behind Copenhagen Street and be there in less than fifteen minutes.'

She was on the move before he'd had a chance to reply, and the Doctor had to hurry to keep up. Moving cautiously, but with as much speed as possible, they made their way swiftly across the city until they were within sight of the Castle. The night was drawing to an end, and the first of the patrols would no doubt soon be marching back to base.

'For someone who's new in town, you seem to have pretty good local knowledge. Or did you get it all from the back of a cereal packet?'

'I've been here long enough.' As she spoke, Emily halted at a junction, checking it was safe to move on. 'First rule of survival – always know where your exits are. Why do you think I chose to take rooms near a city gate?'

The Doctor was impressed. 'Good rule. One of my favourites. Maybe not number one, but definitely up there. Top five at least.'

They stopped momentarily to catch their breath, and the Doctor checked the sky for the first signs of sunrise. 'We have to get inside before dawn breaks. The curfew will be over in less than an hour, and then the Castle will be crawling with soldiers wanting breakfast.'

'Let's hope it isn't us.' Emily joked darkly. 'So what's your plan? Or were you thinking of flashing your little "get out of jail" card again to get us inside?'

The Doctor patted the wallet in his pocket. 'Psychic paper. Never leave home without it. I don't know, sneak in, have a look around. See what turns up.'

'You call that a plan?'

'Works for me,' protested the Doctor. 'Most of the time. What's in the bag, anyway?'

'Essentials.'

'Uh-huh. Packet of chewy mints and the latest Alan Titchmarsh? OK, maybe the chewy mints aren't all that essential but we all love a bit of Alan…'

Emily chose to ignore the Doctor's obscure references. Was he ever serious about anything?

'Binocs, a scanning unit and some field rations. It pays to keep some emergency kit with you, when you're on the run. I thought the binocs might come in useful when we get to the Castle.'

Emily thought it best not to mention the phase pistol she kept reassuringly holstered in the lining of her jacket.

'Hold it,' hissed the Doctor, pulling Emily behind a row

of barrels, as a pair of unhappy-looking soldiers stomped across the street ahead of them, apparently bickering. The Doctor recognised them as the guards from Emily's safe house.

This was bad news. If these men had been sent back to barracks, then their escape had been discovered. Strange that no alarm had been raised, but perhaps the authorities were hoping to avoid the chaos that had followed his arrest earlier in the night. The Doctor strained to hear what they were saying.

'I'm telling you, Hewse, he had official papers. I'm not a complete idiot you know,' Butcher insisted, but his companion was having none of it.

'If the Captain says you are, then who am I to argue? If I end up on latrine duty again because of you, then I'm staying topside, and it's your turn to do the shovelling.'

'Come on, I was in the pit last time…' Butcher complained.

As the grumbling duo moved out of earshot, the Doctor gave Emily a mischievous grin. 'You know, what we really need to get into the Castle is a disguise.'

'You, there. Butcher, isn't it?'

The two soldiers stumbled to a halt as the Doctor stepped out of the shadows ahead of them, blocking their path.

'Oh no, it's him again,' Butcher almost wailed, unhappy at the prospect of yet more trouble.

'Now you listen here. We have reason to believe you

are not who you say you are.' Hewse puffed out his chest, and waggled his pike without much confidence. He wasn't used to confronting authority figures, and he had to admit the tall man had some presence, but there was a chance here to make amends for Butcher's earlier mistake. 'I hereby place you under arrest.'

The Doctor wrinkled his brow in confusion. 'But you've already got me under arrest, haven't you?'

'Oh, yes. Well, back under arrest then,' Hewse spluttered.

'There's obviously been a bit of a misunderstanding here. I think you'll find this parchment should explain everything.' The Doctor held up his wallet, giving both soldiers plenty of time to stare at the blank sheet within. 'Orders from the King. Look, it's got his official seal and everything.'

Butcher and Hewse glanced at each other, knowing they'd seen nothing of the sort but unable to ignore the fact that they were sure they had.

'Even so, the Captain definitely wants a word with you.'

'Yes, yes, I'm sure he does.' The Doctor made a show of slipping his wallet back inside his jacket pocket. Another wallet, the same wallet in fact, appeared as if by magic in his other hand. He handed it to Butcher. 'Actually, I've already had a little chat with the Captain, and he's given me this signed pardon, so we're all good.'

Butcher looked blankly at the psychic paper. He could definitely see words but they meant nothing to him, so he passed it to Hewse, who looked equally nonplussed.

'That could be Captain Darke's signature, I suppose.' He shrugged at the imaginary squiggles. It seemed that, once again, they would have to take the Doctor's word for it. 'Everything seems to be in order, sir,' said Hewse, passing the wallet back to the Doctor, and both soldiers snapped smartly to attention.

'Excellent. Good men. Right then, we'll need your chain mail, your jerkins and your helmets please.'

Butcher and Hewse stared at the Doctor. 'Er, are you sure, sir? I mean, the weather is a bit inclement to be running about in our under-things, sir,' Butcher stammered.

'Captain's orders. It's that or latrine duty…' The Doctor had a feeling that would convince them. 'Oh, and your pikes.' The Doctor turned to Emily. 'Do you think we'll need the pikes?'

Emily nodded in agreement. 'Definitely need the pikes.' She couldn't believe these fools had fallen for the same trick twice. There was no way this species was ever going to break orbit.

'Definitely need the pikes,' confirmed the Doctor to the bemused men.

In unison, they handed over their weapons and began to strip off their armour.

'This isn't going to work,' muttered Emily as they approached the Castle gate. The helmet was too big for her, and she could barely stand under the weight of the chain mail hanging off her shoulders. 'I still don't see why you couldn't use your psychic paper again?'

'There'll be dozens of eyes on us in the Castle. If I have to flash my pass at every single one of them we'll be held up for hours.' The Doctor seemed quite comfortable in his ill-fitting costume. 'Anyway, it'll be fine. You're the very picture of a modern militarian. If anyone stops us, let me do the talking, and if they ask you anything just do your best to look butch and sound gruff.'

'Thanks.' Emily rolled her eyes and marched on.

As it turned out, she needn't have worried. They got through the gate and into the Castle grounds without being challenged.

'I don't think much of their security. A herd of Buntocks could have hopped past and I don't think they'd have noticed.' She sniffed, unimpressed.

'You've got to remember these soldiers have probably been doing double shifts for months. They must be exhausted.' The Doctor paused, lost in thought. 'Now all we have to do is find the Sheriff. I don't suppose you know the layout of this place?'

'I never bothered with it, to be honest. I didn't think I'd ever need to come here. Shouldn't we be looking for the Krillitanes first, anyway?'

'Your average Krillitane is utterly devoted to its leader. As a race they're intellectually advanced, but essentially still very much pack animals, slaves to their tribal heritage. If we're going to stop them, then we need to go straight to the big kahuna.'

'Can we at least ditch these ridiculous uniforms first? How do they breathe in this get-up, let alone fight?' Emily tugged at the neck of her jerkin, which was irritating her skin.

'I thought I looked quite fetching,' said the Doctor, raising the face shield of his helmet and looking around. 'But I suppose it is a bit clangy for covert investigations. Let's dump them and get inside.'

As she struggled free of the hefty metal garment, Emily took the opportunity to take in her surroundings. The Castle was really a collection of one- and two-storey buildings, surrounded by a high fence and a moat. The Sheriff was most likely to be found in the largest of the buildings, she thought, not far from the stables where they were currently hiding.

At the western end of the complex, towards the River Severn, was a high mound upon which stood a stone tower, providing a perfect vantage point for the soldier stationed upon its ramparts to keep a watchful eye over the countryside to the south of the city.

She noted the number of soldiers manning positions along the defences, but it was clear they were too weary to be an effective fighting force. The sense of fatigue in this place was almost palpable, and she wondered what would happen to the morale of the civilian population outside if they were ever to find that out.

'Oi. Are you coming or not?' hissed the Doctor from a doorway in a small extension at the side of the building opposite, and Emily hurried over to join him.

It was a storeroom, though the shelves and barrels inside were desperately in need of restocking. Not only were the soldiers tired, they were hungry too. Pulling the door closed silently, the Doctor put a finger to his lips, warning Emily against speaking, and they moved cautiously towards the sounds of a busy kitchen.

The Doctor peered into the hot, steamy room, the aroma of cooking meat and freshly baked bread assailed his nostrils, and he watched as two women and a young boy busied themselves preparing breakfast for the garrison. They were too engrossed in the task at hand to notice the Doctor and Emily, who slipped silently through the kitchen and into the room beyond. It was a large hall, filled with long tables and benches. At one end, a fire crackled and popped warmly in a large stone hearth.

'The garrison commander would have his quarters on the ground floor, and that's where we'll find our Sheriff,' whispered the Doctor.

This seemed like a reasonable assumption to Emily, but her main concern right now was that if breakfast was almost ready, then half the troops in the Castle might come marching into this very room at any second.

'Well, let's get on with finding it, then,' she said quietly, moving ahead of the Doctor, through an arched opening at the far end of the hall.

She found herself in a wide, candlelit corridor running the length of the building. To the right stood the main doors, one of which was open just enough to allow the cold night air to blow a chilly breeze along the corridor. On the left she could see another set of double doors. That had to be the place.

'There we go. Easy-peasy. Come on.' The Doctor breezed past Emily and headed down the corridor towards the Sheriff's office. 'No guards outside, though. If I was a suspicious man I'd say that was pretty suspicious.'

'Doctor.' Emily's voice was strained, tense, and the Doctor knew immediately that something was wrong.

Turning carefully, the Doctor was dismayed at what he saw.

The shadowy form of a large man gripped Emily tightly, pinning her arms to the sides of her body, pressing the barrel of a phase rifle hard against her temple. Emily's bright eyes were wide with fear.

A gravelly voice rasped out, 'Make one move and she's dead.'

FIVE

'On guard duty as well, Captain? You must be short staffed.' The Doctor spoke quietly, hoping Captain Darke wouldn't do anything stupid.

'I dismissed the guards, Doctor. Otherwise you wouldn't have got this far. In there, please.' Darke nodded towards an open door, and the Doctor entered without question, flashing Emily a reassuring glance as he passed by.

Darke closed the door and pushed Emily towards the Doctor.

'I want the truth this time, Doctor. Who are you, and what is your purpose here? Are you for the King or his enemies?'

'I could ask you the same question. Where did you get that rifle from? The Krillitanes?'

'From under your own floorboards, Doctor,' Darke said plainly. The Doctor glanced momentarily at Emily, sensing her discomfort as she sought to avoid his eyes. 'Or perhaps you are not as well acquainted with your wife as you previously claimed?'

I was right about her then, thought the Doctor, neither disappointed nor surprised. However, now wasn't the time to worry about what was really going on with Emily. He raised his hands and directed his attention towards Darke.

'OK, you're right. Before this evening I didn't know a thing about her, which was probably more than I do now to be honest, but I'm telling you – put down that weapon. You don't know the kind of damage it can do.'

Darke could have laughed. 'Doctor, I've wielded more tools of carnage in my lifetime than you can possibly imagine. All I need to know is that this is the end I point at my target, and this tiny lever is its means of operation.'

The Doctor resisted the urge to throw himself at the soldier and try to wrestle the weapon from Darke's grasp. He had to persuade the Captain that he wasn't a threat, that he was here to help.

'I don't have any answers for you, Captain. None that will make any sense to you, at least not yet. Trust me, what's going on here is far more serious than who controls the throne of England. Put that thing down.'

Despite his reservations, Darke knew this situation was going nowhere unless he allowed himself to afford this oddly attired man a degree of trust. Without another thought, he pushed Emily towards the Doctor, keeping the rifle trained on them both. He was prepared to listen, but there was no point taking silly risks.

'I took this post because I wanted a quiet life. I'm tired of war and fighting. But even here, it seems, in the shire of my birth, I'm unable to escape it. Whether your answers mean anything to me or not, Doctor, I need to know what is happening.'

Emily clung to the Doctor, and he could feel her trembling. 'You OK?' he whispered, eyes fixed on Darke.

Emily nodded meekly, and took a deep breath to regain her composure. 'I'm fine,' she replied, moving away from the Doctor, her voice hard and cold.

The Doctor looked at Darke. The Captain was tired, angry, scared, and in possession of an alien weapon that he was as likely to injure himself with as cause harm to anyone else. The only hope the Doctor had to get all three of them through this unharmed would be to tell Darke the truth, whether he believed it or not. He took a deep breath.

'OK. Here goes. There are monsters here, Captain. Monsters from beyond the stars, that will bring death and destruction upon the world unless I can stop them. It's very possible your Sheriff may be in league with them.'

Darke stared at the Doctor. 'There is nothing beyond the stars save for blackness. No heaven, no monsters. Nothing,' the soldier replied, voice faltering.

'Then explain the deaths.' The Doctor raised an

eyebrow, and let his words hang in the air for a moment. 'They weren't caused by human hand, and there isn't a predator in England capable of hunting such large prey on the wing. The creature that's been killing your people is from a race called the Krillitanes. They're from another world, and I'm going to stop them taking any more innocent lives. So put the gun down, and take me to the Sheriff.'

The Doctor held Darke's stare, and he could sense the soldier's mind reeling at the bizarre notions he'd posited, threatening to be overwhelmed by them. At long last, Darke lowered the rifle.

'What has the Sheriff to do with this?' Darke asked. Since the Sheriff's arrival, he had put his superior's volatile demeanour down to paranoia, but perhaps there was more to it?

'The Krillitanes can disguise themselves, take on human form, and your Sheriff arrived at the same time as the killings started. I could be wrong, but it's a lot of coincidence to ignore. The Sheriff may be one of them.' The Doctor spoke quickly. They didn't have much time. 'He's just along the corridor. Let me speak to him.'

Darke considered the Doctor's words. There was only one way to find out whether there was any truth in them or not. 'You don't need my permission. The Sheriff gave me orders to bring you to him. He is already keen to speak with you himself. He'll be alone. He always is.'

The room wasn't cold but, where earlier a fire had

crackled in the hearth, warming the space, now there were but glowing embers, casting a dim orange light across the walls. The Sheriff stood at the window, back to the door, staring through the tiny crack in the shutters that allowed him to observe the world outside, without ever having to interact with it.

If he'd heard Darke's knock at the door, or chosen to ignore it, the Sheriff didn't seem to notice it creak open. Nor did he move as the Doctor stepped carefully into the room, closely followed by Emily and Darke. In fact, it was difficult to tell if he was even breathing.

'My Lord, I have brought the prisoner, as you commanded.'

No response.

Even for the Sheriff, Darke thought, this behaviour was odd. It seemed quite possible he'd not moved from the window at all, since their conversation in the middle of the night.

'My Lord?' Darke tried again, yet still there was no response.

'Not the chattiest of chaps, is he?' commented the Doctor, watching carefully for any hint of life in the silent figure.

Emily cautiously approached the Sheriff until she was standing beside him. The man's face was expressionless, eyes glazed and vacant. She reached up and brushed his cheek lightly with the back of her fingers.

'He's stone cold,' she said, as the Doctor joined her.

'I'll say. He hasn't even offered us a drink,' he joked

under his breath, frowning. Tapping his tongue against the back of his teeth in thought, the Doctor rolled his eyes towards Emily and fixed a curious and unavoidable gaze upon her. She knew what was coming.

'What would a girl on the run need with a Lokklar-Ri J77 Special Assault sniper rifle with laser-guided optics?' he mused. 'Self defence?' He raised his eyebrows, and Emily found herself feeling lost and guilty.

'What is wrong with him? Is this your doing, Doctor?' Darke interrupted from the other side of the room, and Emily took the opportunity to duck out of the Doctor's line of sight. The Captain was deeply unsettled by the Sheriff's demeanour, unwilling to come any closer.

'Nothing to do with me. He seems to be in some kind of post-hypnotic trance.' The Doctor dug into his coat pockets, retrieving his stethoscope. Warming the chest piece with a quick breath, he carefully placed it against the Sheriff's temple, listening attentively. 'Hardly a spark of electrical activity in the frontal lobe. His brain is just ticking over, like someone picked up the remote control and switched him to standby.'

'He isn't dead, then?' Emily asked.

'No, no, very much alive, just not very lively. Captain Darke, have you ever seen the Sheriff like this before?'

Darke shifted uneasily on his feet. 'Not like this. The men all think he's an odd one, not the man his predecessor was. He spends a lot of time in here, alone. Thinking about it, I don't think I've ever seen him leave this room. But this...?' His voice trailed away, at a loss for words.

Emily tore her attention away from the static figure. 'So, is he a Krillitane or not, Doctor?'

'He's as human as the good Captain here, which rather spoils our little theory. Mind you, he isn't himself either. I think someone's been controlling him.'

The Doctor stuffed the stethoscope away and threw his coat over the Sheriff's unoccupied chair, thinking aloud as he did so. 'Why would the Krillitanes use mind control on a human, when they could just replace him altogether? It's not their style. It just doesn't add up.'

'Can't we wake him up and ask? There's a chance he might know who did this.' The fact was Emily had a fair idea already. A simple interrogation would have made her job easier.

'I shouldn't think he'd remember a thing,' the Doctor pondered. 'The level of control seems pretty deep. Besides, if someone is keeping him on standby, then at some point they're going to switch him back on again. If we've woken him up, they'll know and they'll come after us. Best leave sleeping beauty be, for now.'

All this talk of trances and mind control was beyond Darke's experience, but something was bothering him. 'These monsters you speak of. Did you expect to find more of them at the Castle?'

'Well, they have to be somewhere.' The Doctor shrugged, disappointed that the Castle was looking more like a dead end by the second.

'Doctor, I know this Castle, and every soldier and

civilian within its defences. If there were a force of devilish invaders hiding here, I would know of it.' Of this, if nothing else, Darke could be quite certain.

The Doctor sighed, and walked disconsolately to the shuttered window, leaning around the Sheriff to peer through the crack that so fascinated him.

Dawn had broken, and a soft light was spreading across the cloudless sky. It was going to be a beautiful morning. The snow glistened as the first rays of sunlight touched upon the white tower of the Cathedral, standing tall above the Castle's defences, directly in line with the crack in the shutter.

Directly in line.

The Doctor slammed his palm against his forehead, berating himself for missing the obvious. 'Stupid Doctor. Stupid, silly old Doctor. Oh, I'm losing my touch.'

'What? What is it?' Emily jumped at this sudden, manic change in the Doctor, as he paced the room in excitement.

'The Cathedral. It's been staring us in the face, like a big… Well, like a cathedral. Krillitane or not, that's where the Sheriff is being controlled from. There is a direct line of sight between this room and the Cathedral tower, and I bet if we can get up there we'll find a neural transmitter pointing straight at beardy.'

'Which explains why he never leaves this room.' Emily looked at the Sheriff again. The poor man, his life beyond his own control. It must have been horrible.

'And why we have to get out of here right now,' the

Doctor continued. 'If I'm right, the Sheriff's controllers will do what everyone else does when they get up in the morning.'

'And what's that?'

'They pick up the remote and flick through the channels to see what's been happening in the news.' The Doctor pointed at the Sheriff. 'And he is Natasha Kaplinsky.' He glanced about the room, making sure nothing that might give away their visit was out of place. 'Captain Darke, I need you to do something for me. I know it's a big ask.'

'Doctor, half the things you say make no sense to me, but while I can't explain what has been happening in Worcester these past months, I have a feeling you can. I'm willing to help in any way I am able.'

'Brilliant. Good man. I need you to stay here with the Sheriff, as close as you can without it being obvious. You should be safe, so long as whoever's pulling laughing boy's strings doesn't realise we're onto them. If he does anything out of the ordinary, anything at all, send word to Emily's lodgings.'

Darke nodded. For the first time in many months he felt like he was taking positive action. He felt like a soldier again.

'Oh, and I'll take this. Don't want you accidentally blowing your own head off now, do we?' The Doctor took the sniper rifle from Darke, and quickly stripped it down to its component parts, pocketing the ammo clip and telescopic sight with a flourish.

'Get your skates on, Emily,' he said, as he passed the remaining components to the stunned woman. With that he was off, striding along the corridor towards the main doors, ignoring the confused glances of soldiers filing into the hall for breakfast.

Emily shrugged at Darke, and hurried after him.

By the time she'd caught up, the Doctor was halfway across the wintry compound.

'Where are you going?'

'Up there.' The Doctor pointed enthusiastically, energised by the few pieces of the puzzle that were falling into place. 'The Castle tower. From the top we'll be able to see right into the Cathedral grounds, the Abbey, everything.'

'But the Cathedral is one of the most open places in the city. I've heard the locals talking about how supportive the Bishop has been over the past few months, how helpful.'

'There's an interrogation technique, used all over the galaxy, where law-keepers play off each other to get a confession out of a prisoner. Here they call it "Good Cop/ Bad Cop". Well, they will do one day. Anyway, that's what they're doing here. The Sheriff and the Devil's Huntsman keep the people scared, while the Bishop offers them hope. It's a pretty extreme example, I'll give you that, but what a way of diverting attention from your real base of operations if someone turns up asking awkward questions.'

By now they were inside the tower, racing up its spiral stairs. As they burst into the early daylight, the lone watchman at the top was dismissed with a flash of psychic paper, and the sniper rifle's telescopic sight was back in the Doctor's hand.

'Right then, let's see what we can see.'

The Cathedral was less than a century old, and it's vaulted stonework remained as crisp and sharp as the day its masons had packed away their tools. The pollution of the coming industrial age was yet to eat away at this shining example of medieval craftsmanship, and the Doctor marvelled at the engineering prowess that enabled the construction of such buildings with little more than manpower and faith.

Scanning the tower, he soon found what he was looking for. A small, unobtrusive disc, mounted near a high window. A neural transmitter, as suspected, its emitter array focused squarely on the main building in the Castle grounds.

'There you are. Basic, off-the-shelf hardware, by the look of it. Directional beam, with a limited range. They must've had it primed to take control of the new Sheriff before he'd had time to settle in.'

'Why didn't they just take control of the previous Sheriff?'

'People knew him, they would have noticed he'd changed, whereas the new bloke could be as odd as a limestone muffin and who'd bat an eyelid? Nobody trusts the new boss.'

The Doctor lowered the rifle sight and absently scratched his head. 'Why doesn't any of this seem remotely Krillitaney?'

At the Doctor's shoulder, Emily was also observing the building, scanning across the site with her binocs, watching priests and monks going about their early morning business in the Cathedral grounds. The Doctor could spend as long as he liked searching for answers; the whys and wherefores of the Krillitanes were no concern of hers. Emily knew exactly what she was looking for.

'Like those killings,' the Doctor mumbled, thinking aloud. 'Out in the open, no regard for the consequences. The Krillitanes are usually way more subtle, picking off people who won't be missed, orphans, the homeless, rats. They'd be sorted for rats here. Plenty of rats.'

Emily focused on a group of monks as they were approached by a tall, corpulent priest who had just emerged from the shadows of a doorway.

He spoke to them animatedly, and pointed to the south. Emily squeezed the shutter repeatedly, hoping to get as many of their faces filed on the device's data drive as she could.

She almost dropped it in shock when the alert for a positive ID flashed luridly on the screen.

'They might be bloodthirsty, imperialist villains, but they have a degree of respect for whoever they're invading, even the ones that don't stand a chance.' The Doctor tapped the rifle sight against his chin. What was he missing?

Barely aware the Doctor was still talking, Emily blinked to make sure she wasn't imagining things. Adjusting the controls, she flicked through the image files until she found the correct one.

The message in her display continued to flash, the words blurring as tears threatened to overcome her.

IDENTIFICATION: POSITIVE
TARGET: CONFIRMED

It was the tall priest who had sparked the alert, but the image wasn't quite clear enough for her peace of mind. Snapping back to camera mode, she zoomed in on the big man's fleshy, well-fed face. Despite his relaxed demeanour and avuncular appearance, his eyes were hard, alert, unpleasant. Emily almost laughed to think she'd mistaken the Doctor for this man, they were so very different. She had found him at last. Lozla Nataniel Henk.

Emily felt a hand on her shoulder.

'You're trembling,' said the Doctor, concerned. 'What's wrong?'

'Nothing. Must just be the cold,' Emily lied, turning away, and busying herself returning the binocs to her bag. When she glanced nervously back towards the Cathedral, Henk had gone.

'Emily, if there is anything you need to tell me, anything you know about what's going on here, now would be a good time.'

'I'm sorry, Doctor, I have to go,' she said, pushing past him towards the stairs.

'What? Emily, wait...'

Emily paused at the first step. She could stay, help the Doctor. Finish the job personally. But no, she didn't have the stomach for it. She would leave that to her employers. She looked back over her shoulder, and tried to smile. 'You were right, Doctor, I shouldn't be here. Time to leave.'

A few moments later, as she hurried across the yard and out of the Castle into the awakening city, she could feel the Doctor's concerned eyes following her. Emily didn't look back. If the Doctor wanted to protect this planet from a pack of hungry aliens, that was his business. It was nothing to do with her. She'd done what she had to do, and she wasn't going to stay here any longer.

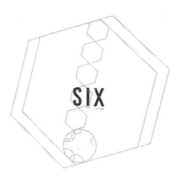

SIX

It had been a bad night for Mister Henk, and he was in no mood for further trouble.

Lynch had been stupid, he'd allowed Toeclaw to get too close, and had paid for it with his life. On the plus side, now Lynch was dead there was one less dividend to be paid out, and the share destined for Henk's own pot would be that bit larger.

Unfortunately, the loss of one man also meant the loss of a more valuable asset. By now, Toeclaw would be dead.

Each of Henk's people had a personal life-signs monitor strapped to their wrist, and the alarm had been raised the instant Lynch's heart had stopped beating. They'd had time to trigger the emergency failsafe, firing a pulse of lethal energy from the inhibitor implant that usually ensured the Krillitane remained under their control. Henk relished the thought of the treacherous creature twisting in pain, crashing to certain death as she fled for her life.

The loss of Toeclaw would be a major problem for the successful completion of the project, but not an insurmountable one. The most important thing as of now was to retrieve her corpse before one of the stunted, semi-evolved natives came across it. That would never do.

Standing in the shadow of the Cathedral, unaware that he was being observed from the Castle tower, Henk addressed the team he'd selected to carry out this mission.

'Find the body and bring it back here. Be discreet, and don't return before nightfall – we need to keep the legend of the Huntsman well and truly alive, so we don't want the locals catching a glimpse of the corpse, do we?'

The four men made noises of agreement and pulled up the hoods of their monks' robes to obscure their faces as they left.

Henk spat a ball of Bacco onto the ground, sniffed disdainfully and went back inside.

Branlo, the spotty young comms technician who had somehow become Henk's right-hand man by default, intercepted him as he stalked through the cloisters.

'Mister Henk, I'm afraid we have another problem.' Branlo paused, nervously, not wanting to make his overbearing boss any angrier than he already was.

'Well, come on. Out with it, lad. I don't imagine one more disaster is going to make very much difference.'

'We recovered Lynch's body…' Branlo stammered. 'It was… He was in a bit of a mess.'

'So would you be if you'd been foolish enough to let one of those ugly monsters get close enough to give you a kiss. What of it?' Henk had no time for prevarication. This was a big day, and so far nothing was going according to plan.

Branlo paused before continuing, his mouth dry. 'His Implant Control Terminal was missing. It wasn't on him or with his personal effects.'

'Why is this a problem? If a native found it, they'll probably use it to ward off some imaginary demon, and if Toeclaw took it, well, she's not going to be using it any time soon, is she?'

'It's just that, I was going through the data from last night, I thought it might help locate Toeclaw's body, and I found this…'

Branlo passed his datapad to Henk. The screen showed a topographical representation of the city, heat signatures from the smallest rats to the groups of soldiers on night patrol. Then, out of nowhere, a phenomenal flash in a quiet part of town.

'An energy spike.' Henk gritted his teeth, and an animal growl began to rise from the depths of his chest. In a flash, he grabbed Branlo by the neck, slamming the terrified technician against a stone pillar, legs dangling a full metre above the tiled floor. 'And no one thought to mention this at the time? Who was on duty?' Henk spat, his fingers tightening around Branlo's throat.

'It was Archa. He was… distracted. It only lasted a millisecond, anyone could have missed it.' Branlo's voice was thin, rasping, he could barely choke out the words.

'Archa? That stimulant-addled waste of space? I knew he was a liability.' Henk released his grip, letting Branlo drop to the floor, where the boy coughed, gasping for air, wishing he'd followed his father's advice and gone into racketeering.

'There's more,' Branlo croaked. 'Shortly after the spike, we get heat readings on someone non-Terran in exactly the same spot. Two hearts, look. It's possible they found the controller…' He lifted his datapad weakly in Henk's direction.

'I'm not interested in possibilities, Branlo. I want facts. Find out where our visitor went next, and tell Archa I'm taking back two percentage points from his dividend.' Branlo nodded as he dragged himself painfully to his feet, but Henk hadn't finished. 'Someone teleported in last night, and if they turn out to be hostile then tell Archa he'll be getting one final dividend cut from me, and I mean very final. Get out of my sight.'

Branlo scurried away, glad to have been dismissed with nothing worse than a bruised neck.

Henk thundered into the nave.

More bad news. It seemed that despite a rigorous recruitment process, he had surrounded himself with amateurs. Now there was this unexpected and unannounced arrival, despite the extensive precautions he'd taken to ensure that only invited guests could find their way to this planet. There would be time to look into it himself soon enough. First, though, he had to make sure the stock hadn't been disturbed by the recent turn of events.

Stopping by a door at the foot of a short flight of steps, he retrieved a set of heavy keys from the depths of his robes. Henk selected one and pushed it into an iron mortise lock that kept the entrance to the crypt secure. The mechanism clunked reassuringly, and he stepped into the darkness beyond.

Another flight of stone steps led to a small antechamber, dimly lit by the screens of a monitoring station and a desk lamp. Belima Febron, a middle-aged, blue-skinned Velurian woman in medical overalls, looked up from her book at the sound of the visitor.

'Mister Henk. I trust you've not uncovered any more murdered staff this morning?' She smiled.

'The day is young, my dear, and my patience has already been sorely tested. By lunchtime, I may have murdered a few of them myself.' Henk was almost joking. He liked Febron. She wasn't afraid of him, which made conversation so much more tolerable. Furthermore, it was her genius that had made this project possible, and would soon make him very, very rich.

'How are our guests?' Henk peered at the grainy images on the monitors. It was difficult to distinguish between what were merely shadows among the stone pillars and the dark, crooked shapes hanging from the ceiling.

Febron leaned past Henk, and touched the largest screen, dragging the view of one security camera to the main area. The life-sign data immediately populated an area to the left-hand side, and even Henk's untrained eye could tell they were fluctuating wildly.

'They're always unsettled when the dominant female is taken out, but this one seems to have realised her return is overdue. I've increased the suppressant dosage, but he's one of the more productive specimens. I don't want to push it too far.'

'Still, we don't want him agitating the others.' Henk went to the small cabinet beside the door that separated this room from the crypt, and pulled out a long plastichrome pole. As he thumbed the activation switch on its grip, the other end of the pole sprang into life, sparks of plasmic charge jumped between electrodes at its tip. 'Open the door, if you'd be so kind.'

Febron did so, and followed Henk into the crypt proper, past rows of heavy, breathing shapes in the half-darkness all around them. Unit twelve was the only beast Henk was concerned with: 'Broken Wing' as the men had nicknamed him, after they'd shattered the main cartilage in his left wing as he'd desperately fought to evade capture.

Henk stopped just before the silent Krillitane. Its wings wrapped tightly about its body like a cocoon.

'You're not sleeping. I can tell. I can see you tremble.'

he said, softly, unconcerned, taunting. 'You know she's dead, don't you, your Brood Mother? She crossed a line, so we fried her brain.'

With a roar of impotent rage, Broken Wing's back suddenly arched, and he twisted towards Henk, teeth bared, snapping open and closed.

Henk didn't flinch, watching calmly as the creature writhed before him, spitting and snarling, arms restricted by thick chains binding wrists to ankles, by pipes, wires and cables snaking away from its body towards the silent, blinking technology.

'Now, now,' Henk admonished, raising the plasma lance and casually increasing its power discharge. His eyes glistened, maliciously, in the white light of its sparking tip. 'If you won't behave, Daddy will have to punish you.'

Febron quietly turned and made her way back to the antechamber, ignoring the agonised screech of the Krillitane male echoing amongst the pillars.

'That should cool Broken Wing's temper for the foreseeable,' Henk sniffed, deactivating the lance and replacing it in its locker.

Working at the monitoring station, Febron busied herself fine-tuning the delicate balance of stimulants and sedatives flowing into the now unconscious Krillitane. 'He'll live, but his productivity is going to suffer. Did you have to go quite so far?'

'I've already lost one member of staff. If the stock get

it into their heads that we're weak, then more of them will attempt to follow in Toeclaw's footsteps. Now they'll think twice,' he told her, slamming the locker door shut to emphasise his point. 'We're close enough to the end of this phase of the project to temporarily take a hit in production levels.'

'I'm more worried about the tour. You don't really expect me to do a presentation, do you?' The scientist was genuinely dreading the prospect.

Henk chuckled. 'You lend gravitas, my dear. Authority, scientific integrity, and you could charm the tentacles off an Octulan.'

Febron sighed. There would be no getting out of this. 'It's not their tentacles I'm worried about. When do the first delegates arrive?'

'They should all have arrived by this evening, all being well. We've already received a coded signal from our Calabrian friends. They will be making planetfall in a matter of hours.'

Picking up her book and settling back in her chair, Febron smiled at Henk. 'Let's just hope we don't have any further mishaps along the way then, eh?'

'You keep your mind on keeping things ticking over down here, and I'll worry about the bigger picture.' Henk patted the scientist softly on her shoulder. 'Now, if you'll excuse me, I need to make a quick call.'

'Do you mind if I join you?'

Captain Darke had been picking at a plate of lukewarm

meat and dry bread on the table before him with little interest, and turned at the familiar voice to find the Doctor standing behind him, looking distracted.

'Where's your friend?' The Captain glanced around for the pretty young woman, and was surprised at the disappointment he felt when he couldn't see her.

'Emily? She's gone. It's better that way,' replied the Doctor, but Darke sensed his companion's concern for the girl. The Doctor nodded in the vague direction of the Sheriff's quarters. 'How's cheerful Charlie? Still the life and soul?'

'He remains in his waking sleep. There didn't seem much point in staying with him, so I posted a guard outside and decided to get something to eat.' Darke prodded the chunks of food around his plate for the umpteenth time. 'Funny thing, though. I've not eaten for the best part of a day, yet I find I no longer have any appetite.'

'Captain, the Sheriff wishes to see you.'

The unexpected new voice brought him out of his reverie. He hadn't noticed the guard come over, and Darke felt his stomach tighten. The Sheriff was awake.

'Of course. You can finish this if you like.' Darke pushed the plate of food towards the Doctor, who immediately tore off a strip of bread and popped it in his mouth nonchalantly.

Darke rose from the table and made his way to the Sheriff's quarters. Before he'd had a chance to knock, he heard the Sheriff's voice.

'No need to announce your presence, Captain. You may enter.'

The Sheriff was sitting at his desk, with no outward sign to suggest he'd done anything other than have a good night's sleep. 'Unless I'm much mistaken, I believe I gave you orders to bring your prisoner to me.'

'I assumed you'd prefer to wait until morning, my Lord, allow the prisoner time to get some rest, so he could better answer your questions,' Darke bluffed. 'He remains in his lodgings on the other side of town.' It was the best excuse he could think of. He had no intention of revealing that the Doctor was in this very building, and the lie would buy them some time.

'I think it's best if you follow orders and leave the thinking to your superiors, don't you?' sneered the Sheriff, and Darke wondered if he was equally repugnant when his mind was his own.

'I received further intelligence during the night, concerning your prisoner. It seems he may be from out of town. Therefore my need to speak with him has become more pressing.' The Sheriff paused, and it struck Darke that it was almost as if the man were listening to some other voice, whispering in his ear. 'Send an armed guard. It is imperative that the prisoner is not allowed to escape.'

'Of course, my Lord, I understand. I shall fetch him myself, straight away.' Darke bowed and left the Sheriff to his own or, more likely, somebody else's dark thoughts.

***

The sensation of engaging with the world through someone else's eyes, forcing your thoughts and words through their mouth, was something unique, and Henk relished every moment. True, his control over the Sheriff was limited, but to feel another being's soul subsumed beneath one's own was one hell of a rush.

Henk disengaged the neural relay, casually removing the headset and tossing it onto the table. He relaxed back into the Bishop's ornate chair, knowing that the Sheriff would have reverted to a sleep state already. The human probably wouldn't last much longer – direct mind control without suitable recovery periods was fatal – but the Sheriff was an expendable tool, and the project was nearing completion.

The hidden scanners would alert him to the arrival of the prisoner, giving Henk plenty of time to reconnect with his puppet Sheriff, and he would make short work of the prisoner if he turned out to be a threat.

He felt sure his Krillitanes would enjoy the extra meal.

The Captain closed the door behind him, softly. What had the Sheriff meant by 'further intelligence'? What's more, when had he received it?

Darke looked at the guard he'd posted outside the chamber. 'You're certain the Sheriff has received no visitors?' he demanded.

'None, sir,' said the man.

Darke was certain that nobody could have gained

an audience with the Sheriff without the soldier seeing them, which meant that no one else had been in the room since he'd spent the early hours in there with the Doctor, Emily and the strangely distant Sheriff.

If an external force was controlling the Sheriff, that had to be where he had got his new information from, transferred directly into his mind by whoever it was within the Cathedral that held dominion over his thoughts and actions. If they wanted to capture the Doctor, then they had decided that he was a threat, and Darke had to find him and warn him.

He hurried back into the main hall, but stopped short. The room was empty, save for a half-empty plate at the table where they had been sitting minutes earlier. There was no sign of the Doctor.

Ignoring a rising tide of panic, Darke hurried briskly to the main doors, and out into the snow-covered yard, wincing in the bright sunlight as he scanned for the Doctor. What was the man playing at? Where could he have gone?

The answer was right there in front of him. The Cathedral. The mad fool was going in there, alone, unprotected.

Darke broke into a run, out of the Castle and into the now busy Worcester streets, pushing his way through the early morning bustle, desperately looking ahead for a glimpse of the Doctor's tall form.

Finally, in the distance, there he was, striding into the Cathedral grounds as if he owned the place. Darke knew there was no way he was going to catch him in time, but he upped his pace regardless.

'Doctor, wait,' he shouted, turning the heads of a few passers-by, no doubt wondering what all the fuss was about. But it was too late. He could do nothing but watch as the doors of the Cathedral closed behind the Doctor.

SEVEN

Emily smiled at the tumbledown barn ahead of her. The roof was bowed, and its timber sides battered and cracked. It would offer scant protection against the elements, and looked as if it would collapse if she stared at it too hard for too long.

As cloaking devices went, the simplicity of the upgraded system on her ship was breathtaking. For a fraction of the cost of showy invisibility cloaks, it just meshed the ship's shields with a holographic projection system, selecting a suitably innocuous disguise based on local architecture which blended in but was utterly impenetrable. She couldn't think why nobody had come up with something like it before.

Activating the security overrides, Emily opened a portal in the shield and stepped aboard the compact vessel she called home. As she entered the access corridor to the main cabin, lights flickered on, along with the low hum of the life support powering up.

'Welcome aboard,' purred an electronically synthesized female voice.

'Hello, Babe,' Emily addressed the shipboard AI, glad to hear a reassuringly familiar voice, however digitally synthesized it was. 'Engage the long-range transmitter, please.'

She dumped her rucksack on the cabin floor and pulled out her binocs, plugging them into the ship's data terminal with practised efficiency.

'Ten-point encryption, via a narrow beam. I don't want anyone listening in.' Emily ordered, her hands tapping at the terminal keys, uploading images of Henk and his associates to the message she was preparing to fire out into the galaxy, along with an invoice. She would wait for a response, and for payment to reach her preferred bank, before blasting off this rock and heading who knew where. 'OK, Babe. Message is bundled. Please transmit and monitor for response.'

'Confirmed.'

Babe. What a stupid name for a shipboard AI, thought Emily. It would be easy enough to change, the AI certainly didn't care what she called it, but she'd become used to it now, and besides it was a reminder of happier times.

Emily relaxed back into her seat, suddenly exhausted, aching for sleep. She'd expected to feel elated, having achieved what she'd set out to, but strangely she felt only emptiness. The void in her heart had not been filled, just thrown into stark relief.

Then there was the guilty feeling that she'd betrayed the Doctor, leaving him to the not so tender mercies of Mister Henk. This crazy stranger, who seemed to want nothing more than to get himself mixed up in things that weren't his business, to help for the sake of helping. The Doctor could look after himself. Couldn't he?

The space inside any religious temple demanded a degree of reverence, even from the most hardened non-believer, and this was especially true of the European cathedrals of this era. The Doctor relaxed and let the silence wash over him, drinking in the splendid calm of the nave. He stared up towards the vaulted ceiling high above, its stonework stretching out like the fine bones in a bird's wing. Now, unfortunately, wasn't the time for architectural appreciation. He had some serious rooting around to do. But where to begin?

The slap of sandalled footfalls on the cold marble floor caught the Doctor's attention, and he saw a monk scurry out from behind a pillar at the quire end of the nave, moving quickly towards a stone doorway.

'Perfect.' The Doctor smiled, then raised his voice, surprised at the power the acoustics lent it. 'Hello! D'you think you could help me?'

The surprised monk spun around and froze at the unexpected voice, looking like a startled rabbit staring out of a hessian sack.

The Doctor ambled over to the monk, speaking quickly and authoritatively, not giving him a chance to get a word in edgeways. 'I've been sent to carry out an audit of ecclesiastical accoutrements in the local environs. You should have received a notification parchment from… Ofcom. Actually, is the Bishop about? He'll be expecting me.'

The monk's shocked expression didn't fill the Doctor with confidence, and for a moment he worried that he might have overplayed the chirpiness. 'Oh blimey, you haven't taken a vow of silence have you? You have, haven't you? That's going to make things awkward when it comes to filling out the questionnaire.'

'Brother Matthew was rendered dumb at an early age, I'm afraid. A terrible accident. While a sad affliction for him, it is a great asset to his order.' A strong voice echoed from the opposite side of the Cathedral, where a tall man with sharp, intelligent eyes met the Doctor's gaze. 'Perhaps I can be of assistance? I am the Bishop of the Diocese. Bishop Henk.'

'Course you are. Bishop Henk, hello, I'm the Doctor. I was just telling old Brother Matthew here…'

'Yes, I overheard your conversation. The sound carries in this wonderful building. You can continue about your good works now, Brother Matthew.' The monk bowed nervously, and scurried past the Doctor, careful to keep his hooded face obscured. Bishop Henk continued, with a tight smile. 'A survey of some kind, you say? On behalf of?'

The Doctor noticed a hint of tension in the Bishop's voice. 'My master, Baron Urnnold, the Burgess of the county of Worcestershire. King Stephen is demanding an increase in levies, so we're exploring all available revenue streams: stocks of gold, arms, comestibles. I'm doing cathedrals and churches, my colleague got inns and taverns. Needless to say, it's taking him longer to work through his list. Still, mustn't grumble. *Allons-y.*'

'Quite so. Of course, we'll be happy to give you any assistance we can.' Henk gave a slight bow, but his keen eyes continued to regard the Doctor, unsure what to make of this random visitor.

'So, Bishop *Henk*,' the Doctor placed specific emphasis on the name, 'when did you come and take over here? Last I heard, Worcester had a bishop by the name of Simon.'

'The previous incumbent was fortunate enough to receive a sudden Papal invite. He left for Rome immediately.' The Bishop spoke calmly. 'I am merely a factotum, until a permanent replacement can be found.'

'Well, I hear you're very popular amongst the townsfolk. A bright light in these dark times. Who knows, maybe you'll get the job full-time.'

'It would be an honour to serve, to be sure. But what of you, Doctor? I take it you are a recent visitor to this fair city?'

'Very much so. In fact I just got here, yesterday evening to be precise. Almost came a cropper of this curfew business, though. Apparently there was some kerfuffle and they made an arrest. Terrible monster loose in the shire, causing no end of fuss, they say. Do you know anything about it?'

The Bishop replied, evasively. 'We keep ourselves to ourselves here, and leave the business of maintaining law and order to the professionals. I'm sure the Sheriff knows exactly what he's doing.'

'I wouldn't be so sure,' the Doctor murmured, as he breezily wandered over to a rather beautiful fresco. 'Anyway, no time like the present. Maybe we could tot up your idols first, then move on to candlesticks?'

He grinned at Bishop Henk, who smiled back wanly.

A good forty-five minutes later, Henk was clearly beginning to wonder if his visitor was little more than an itinerant lunatic, using his wit to get out of the cold.

For his part, the Doctor had been diligently sketching and scribbling furiously in a leather-bound notebook, maintaining his cover as an auditor while testing the supposed Bishop with sly questions about medieval life. As expected, he'd found numerous gaps and inaccuracies in the man's knowledge. Not knowing the name of the current Pope had been a bit of a blinder, considering he was posing as a Bishop. Henk hadn't even batted an eyelid when the Doctor casually mentioned Pope Delboy.

The Doctor was satisfied that this was no human he was speaking to, but equally he was no Krillitane.

By now, they had almost completed a circuit of the nave, and it looked like Henk had had enough. He was about to usher the Doctor out of the Cathedral altogether when a young monk rushed in from the cloisters.

The youngster immediately noticed the Doctor, and hurriedly buried the datapad he was carrying inside his robes. 'Bishop Henk, your worshipfulness, if I could beg a moment of your time,' stammered the youth.

Henk looked more than happy at the interruption. 'Of course, Brother Branlo. Please forgive me, Doctor, but I have church matters to attend to. Would you excuse me for a moment?'

'Oh, of course. Go right ahead. I'll just carry on auditing. I'm quite happy on my own. It's a solitary old business, being an auditor. Maybe I should become a monk, eh? Better social life.'

'Yes, I suppose it must be,' said Henk, and all but dragged Branlo out of the nave.

In the safety of the cloisters, away from the babbling idiot, Henk smiled at Branlo. 'It's a good job you came along. It wouldn't do for the Bishop to be caught throttling a member of his congregation. What did you find out?'

Branlo looked from Henk and back towards the direction of the nave. 'Erm, a box, sir. I mean, I took some of the men to the location of the energy spike we detected, and there was a box there. Only, it was giving out some extremely odd energy readings. I think it must be a teleport terminal or something. I put it under guard, just in case anyone tried to return to it.'

'Good work, Branlo. I'm impressed.'

'But there's more, sir.' Branlo again glanced nervously towards the doorway to the nave.

Henk frowned, and followed his gaze. 'What is it, boy? Why can you never get to the point?'

'Sorry sir. I left a diagnostic running on the Bio-Scanner, tracking the double pulse that came out of the box. Anyway, it settled for a bit, but it's hardly stopped moving since Lynch was killed. Until now.' Branlo swallowed, and stared at the entrance to the nave.

'Oh.' Henk's eyes opened wide in realisation, annoyed at himself for not recognising the idiot auditor as an imposter sooner. 'I wish I'd throttled him after all.'

'Not good.' The instant the door closed behind Henk and the new arrival, the Doctor knew he was in trouble. They were onto him.

He was too far from the main door to make a run for it, and the only other way out was through the very cloisters to which the faux bishop had just departed. The only option was to hide and figure out an escape route later.

Then he remembered a door he'd noticed earlier, hidden down a short flight of steps that they had wandered past twenty minutes earlier. Henk had paid it no attention. Perhaps he didn't even know it was there.

The Doctor sped across the short distance to the dark oak door, but it was deadlock sealed. With no time to wonder why, he dug frantically through his pockets, pulling out an old French picklock. 'Forgotten I had that.

Really should get it back to Marie Antoinette next time I see her.' He thrust the intricate tool into the lock, turning it delicately until he heard a reassuring clunk as the lock's internal mechanism shifted. In a flash he ducked inside, pulling the door closed quietly behind him. He took a moment to lock it again, before kissing the picklock and slipping it back in his pocket.

Glancing around, he saw he was in a small, windowless chamber, probably an antechamber to the crypt, and it wasn't as dark as it should have been.

'Hello. That shouldn't be here.' The blinking lights of a computer terminal made the Doctor's hearts sink. Not such a good hiding place after all, but seeing as he was stuck in here for now, he might as well make the most of it and explore.

Popping on his glasses, the Doctor settled into an empty chair in front of the incongruous bank of high technology, and cast his eyes over its array of monitor screens. One of these cycled through grainy, indistinct footage from security cameras, while another flickered with cardiovascular readings and nutrient-flow levels. But for what?

A flash of movement caught his eye, drawing the Doctor's attention back to the security camera. A white coat swept across the screen and was gone, leaving a view of dark shadows and columns. The crypt, and someone was in there.

The Doctor operated the control unlocking the steel door which separated the antechamber from the crypt, and it opened with a soft hiss. He slipped through as stealthily as possible. The first thing that hit him was the smell, like that of a zoo, a mixture of sweat and muck and enclosures. Then there was the unusual bubbling hum, emanating from all around him in the darkness, as if fluid were being pumped by a dozen tiny turbines.

He became aware of heavy shapes, hanging silently between the crypt's many pillars, of cables snaking across the floor, of the quiet rhythm of sleeping bodies breathing. He'd been in a place like this before. A school in London, eight hundred and a bit years in the future. Then there had been a quick and easy exit, but this time he was trapped. With nowhere else to go, he might as well carry on.

Moving cautiously between the shapes he now knew to be sleeping Krillitanes, he could see a brighter area ahead, where a woman in a white lab coat was standing beneath a limp, battered Krillitane, its wings drooped and brushing the floor.

The Doctor stopped a short way behind the woman, and cleared his throat to get her attention. To his surprise, she continued to tend to the creature's wounds.

'What is it? Can't you see I'm busy?' she snapped, without turning.

'Nothing really, I just wondered what you were doing?'

With one swift movement, Belima Febron was facing the Doctor, a gun in her hand pointing straight at his chest. 'Who the hell are you?'

'Nobody special. And shouldn't you keep your voice down? Krillitanes are very light sleepers, you know.'

'They're sedated. I decide when, and if, they wake up. Tell me who you are, or I'll shoot you stone dead.'

'The Doctor,' boomed Henk's voice from the darkness. There was a clunk as a heavy switch was pulled, and bright lamps flickered on, their harsh light casting angular shadows across every surface. 'Thank you, Belima. I'll take care of things from here.'

Henk was accompanied by Branlo and two thickset lumps of men, who lumbered over and grabbed the Doctor by his arms.

'Oi, watch the suit. They're a bit heavy-handed for men of the cloth, aren't they?'

'You're either a genius or a lunatic, Doctor, or perhaps some combination of the two. How long did you think you could get away with your little deception?'

'Long enough.' The Doctor took advantage of the sudden light, and the clear view it afforded of his surroundings. The crypt ran the length of the western end of the Cathedral, filled with pillars bearing the weight of the marble floor above. Each pillar was about two metres distant from its neighbour, and between each group of four hung an individual Krillitane, ankles clamped securely to a strengthened brace, arcing across a metal framework. But this wasn't the only point of contact between technology and Krillitanes. Wires curled around muscles and sinews, electrodes pierced leathery skin, sharp clamps bit into wings, literally clipping them, and a tight aluminium collar forced their chins up at an unnatural angle, allowing tubes to penetrate glands otherwise hidden behind the bones of their lower jaws.

It was an ugly, brutal sight.

'What is this place?' the Doctor breathed, disgusted and horrified at the conditions the creatures were being held in.

'Rather impressive, don't you think? How do you like my Krillitane farm?'

'What? Farm!' The Doctor couldn't believe what he was hearing. 'You can't "farm" a sentient life form. Not even the unpleasant ones. What are you hoping to get out of them? Wool? You'll have a long wait. They out-evolved the need for protective body hair millennia ago.'

'You know something of Krillitane biology, then? Excellent. You should talk with my scientific adviser here.' Henk smiled at the blue-skinned scientist, who replied with a modest, grateful bow. 'Professor Belima Febron is the galaxy's foremost expert on the species. I'm sure you'd be fascinated at some of the discoveries she has made – with my financial support, of course.'

'Then she must realise you can't hold Krillitanes under these conditions. Whatever the ethical objections, they won't just sit back and accept it.' Things were finally beginning to make some degree of sense to the Doctor. The Krillitane he had encountered last night had obviously been one of Henk's. 'You've already lost one, haven't you? What happened? Did it slip its lead while it was being taken out for walkies?'

'We allow them some free-range time. We've found their oil is so much purer when they have enjoyed the thrill of the hunt, and it is their oil that provides the foundation for all our work.' Henk had wandered over to the alcove where Broken Wing was hanging unconscious, and gazed upon it disdainfully. 'Unfortunately the Brood Mother evaded her handler, but she has been dealt with. Rest assured, we are well aware of the Krillitanes' nature and have taken great pains to devise a system of emergency measures in the event of just such an occurrence. It won't happen again.'

So that's what all this was about. Krillitane Oil. A secretion generated by glands in their necks. That explained the pipes and the unsettling gurgling noise of fluid being drained. But what were this mad scientist and her banker extracting it for? 'You don't run a chip shop do you? Krillitane Oil is great for frying chips. Really tasty.'

'No more questions, Doctor. At least, not from you.' Henk sniffed, and caught Febron's eye. She nodded back, knowing what to do.

The Doctor felt an ice-cold rush in his neck, and woozily realised that the scientist had injected him with a sedative. That really wasn't fair. Just when he was getting somewhere. Oh well. He could do with a nap anyway...

He sagged, unconscious, in the arms of his captors.

EIGHT

Eyes blinked open, sweeping away the residue of unconsciousness, and the familiar recessed lighting and white panelling of the ceiling above finally resolved into focus. The soft ringing alarm wasn't showing any sign of ceasing, though.

With a sigh, Emily swung her legs over the side of her bunk and dropped lightly to the deck, the shock of cold metal against her feet helping to shake off the last vestiges of sleep. Not that she'd slept particularly well. Her dreams had all ended in some form of hideous death for the Doctor, and the chimes of the comms alarm were a welcome excuse to wake up.

'Babe, I'm awake. You can turn off the alarm now. Just show me the message.'

'Transmitting to Comms Terminal now,' cooed the

shipboard AI's gentle voice. Emily quickly read the brief transmission. Her data on Henk had been received and verified, and payment credited. No word of thanks, or even an indication of who had actually been paying her. Not that it mattered. This job had been a one-off, passed on to her by a family friend, which she'd taken solely because Henk had been the target. She didn't care where the money had come from.

The message signed off with an odd footnote. 'Our client has informed us that agents have been despatched and will arrive in one solar day. You would therefore be advised to leave prior to their arrival.'

It read like a warning. Or was it a threat? Either way, it was none of her business any more.

Emily was about to head into the cockpit to begin the prep cycle for launch, when she caught sight of her rucksack, and the disassembled barrel of her sniper rifle jutting out of it at an angle. Once again she felt a pang of guilt. 'Aw, rats and barnacles,' she sighed, slumping resignedly into the terminal's flight seat. It was no good. Much as she'd tried to convince herself she had the chops to be a hard-nosed bounty hunter, the truth of the matter was that she was way out of her depth, and her conscience wouldn't allow her to simply cut and run without at least warning the Doctor that being anywhere near Henk had just became a whole heap more dangerous.

Within thirty minutes, Emily was kitted up and on the move, cutting across country to make up for lost time.

It was early afternoon, and the bright, clear skies of the morning had been obscured by ominous, heavy clouds, threatening to coat the landscape with another layer of thick snow before nightfall.

Emily hurried on, trudging through a copse of scrubby woodland, mindful that she had limited time to make the round trip, and vainly hoping that the Doctor would be where she'd left him.

So focused was she that she didn't notice a shapeless heap ahead of her, partially buried in a small drift of snow, until she all but tripped over it.

'Oh gods,' Emily gasped and stumbled backwards, clinging to the trunk of a tree, covering her mouth to ward off the urge to vomit. Alert and terrified, she scanned the woodland around her, but there was nothing to be seen except the dense expanse of trees and branches. An army could be hiding out there and she wouldn't have been able to see them.

After taking a moment to regain her composure, Emily steeled herself to examine the remains of the body on the ground before her.

It – she – had been a humanoid female. Her left arm was dislocated, wrenched at a hideous angle, and there was a jagged tear across her midriff. The dead woman's eyes stared emptily towards the sky, as her blood saturated the snow, steam drifting lazily from the open wound.

The body was still warm. This was a recent kill.

Emily took a closer look at the poor woman's face,

and immediately noticed the ridge of cartilage along the bridge of her nose and at the base of her forehead. An alien, then. A Calabrian? What was a Calabrian woman doing out here in the woods? Apart from being murdered. Maybe she was another one of Henk's people?

His staff seemed to have a pretty high mortality rate, she thought morbidly.

Snap.

A noise right behind her, a twig breaking. Before Emily had a chance to react, a rough hand grabbed her under her chin, while another twisted her arm painfully behind her back.

'Get your hands off me,' Emily shouted, kicking out as she was lifted from the floor, her boot connecting with the knee of a second assailant, who crumpled to the floor, shouting a string of expletives as he fell.

'I've got her. Get the neck brace on, before she gets a chance to shape shift.'

Emily saw a third man rush towards her, a large, painful-looking collar in his hands. They were all wearing monks' robes. Henk's men. Probably the same ones she'd seen outside the Cathedral. They must have been with the Calabrian.

'I didn't kill her. This is nothing to do with me.' She struggled, but the man's grip was too tight.

'You should be dead,' growled the rough voice of her captor, his breath hot against her ear.

The one she'd floored with her wild kick had recovered himself, and was storming towards her, eyes blazing. He lashed out with the back of his hand, slapping Emily hard. 'That was for Lynch,' he snarled.

Emily screwed her eyes shut, waiting for the next punch, but none came. She half-opened her eyes to find a fourth figure, holding a portable scanner in her direction.

'This isn't her.'

'What do you mean? Of course it's her. Who else would've killed the Calabrian?'

'I'm telling you, this isn't Toeclaw.' The monk was agitated, scared. He pulled out a blaster, pointing it wildly in every direction. 'That Krillitane witch is still out there.'

Without warning, something heavy and powerful, crashed into the clearing from above. Twigs and branches scattered to the ground all around Emily, and suddenly the grip of her captor loosened. Emily looked around wildly, trying to make sense of what was happening. The monk with the blaster lay, unmoving, a few metres away, his neck obviously broken.

She looked up as a scream echoed through the woodland. A grey, indistinct shape leapt agilely from tree trunk to branch, chasing down one of Henk's monks as he fled in blind panic. The poor man didn't stand a chance.

Emily had no intention of hanging around to find out what happened next. Pausing long enough to retrieve the monk's blaster, she ran in the opposite direction, as fast as she'd ever run in her life. There could be no doubt that she had just witnessed the awesome power of a Krillitane.

A distant howl echoed through the woods, impossible to locate. Emily heard two men shouting instructions at each other, and then, inevitably, a strangled scream.

Emily began to sob between gulps of air, realising that there was no hope of escaping. She'd had a chance to leave, why hadn't she taken it? Her footsteps began to falter, and she stumbled, reaching out to grab a branch for support. She clung to the tree, panting, tears streaming down her face.

Then, with a sickening thump, the battered, lifeless body of a monk smashed into undergrowth nearby, its passage interrupted by a tree trunk. Emily gasped, unwilling to look at the body, its spine wrapped unnaturally around the tree. Then she sensed a presence, approaching from behind, the creature that was about to snuff out her life.

'You are not one of Henk's people, are you?' came an unexpected voice.

Emily turned, slowly. Standing there was a Calabrian woman. Impossibly, the same woman whose body she had discovered just minutes earlier.

'No,' she replied, surprised at the resolve in her voice. 'I'm nothing to do with that monster.'

The Calabrian woman studied Emily for a moment, head cocked to one side, like a hunter sizing up its prey. 'Then perhaps you would help me kill him.'

***

Eyes blinked open, sweeping away the residue of unconsciousness, and an unfamiliar stone ceiling finally resolved into focus. A thumping headache continued to bang away at his frontal lobe, and it wasn't showing any sign of fading. There was no way of knowing how long he'd been out of it, but it could easily have been a few hours.

The Doctor was in the antechamber to the crypt, tied securely to a chair near the monitoring station. Febron, the brains behind the brawn of this very dodgy set-up, was busy making adjustments to the various systems that ran through it, her back turned towards him.

'It's not very sporting, is it, really? Sticking a great big hypo in someone's neck when they're not expecting it,' the Doctor complained. 'You could've given me some advance warning. I mean, had I known, I could have adjusted my physiology to counteract whatever tranquiliser you pumped into me, mitigate its effects. But no, bang, squidge, bleugh.' He lolled his head back, dangling his tongue, but Febron took no notice of his little piece of theatre.

'Then again, what kind of cunning malevolent genius would warn someone when they were about to knock them out?' The Doctor sniffed and shook his head vigorously to clear it. 'Aw, what was that stuff, anyway? Ropivacaine? Fentanyl? My tongue feels like I've been licking envelopes for three months. Did you have to?'

Febron finally spoke, impatiently and without casting him a backward glance. 'You should have been unconscious for three months, considering the dosage I gave you.' She finished what she was doing, and sat on the edge of the desk, arms crossed, apparently now ready to engage in conversation.

'You know, you have a fascinating biology, Doctor. I've never seen anything quite like it.'

'Make the most of it. You'll never come across another one quite like mine.' As the Doctor spoke, he quietly tested the ropes that bound him to the chair, but was disappointed to find them expertly fastened. If he'd had a grain of sand for every time he'd been tied up over the years, he'd probably have enough by now to form a comfy retirement planetoid in the Bournemouth Cluster. Not that he was planning on hanging up his trainers quite yet.

'Anyway, ignoring my fascinating biology, your boss thought we should have some fun talking Krillitane, so let's talk Krillitane. You been torturing them for long?'

'Firstly, Mister Henk is not my boss. He's merely my financial backer—'

'Sounds like a boss to me,' interrupted the Doctor, but Febron ignored him.

'And secondly I'm a scientist, not a butcher. My Krillitanes are being held under laboratory conditions. Their natural proclivity towards hunting demands that they are kept under lock and key, as much for their own safety as ours.'

'Laboratory conditions, eh? Funny that, because I could've sworn Henk called it a "farm".'

Febron smiled icily. 'Perhaps not the word I would have chosen, but Mister Henk has a weakness for a colourful turn of phrase. Our project is a scientific and commercial venture, something rather more special than merely agricultural.' She paused, possibly concerned that she'd revealed too much. 'However, none of this is your concern.'

The Doctor watched her move away, but he wasn't going to let the conversation end there. 'Well, it is my concern, you see, because I've got a bit of a soft spot for this little planet, and I'm not overly happy with any bunch of suits and scientists who think it's OK to dump a herd of ruthless imperialist carnivores on it.'

'You've no need to worry. Once our business here is completed, we'll be in a position to create a purpose-built facility on a less developed world.'

'So, why here? Why Earth? If you plan to set up somewhere else anyway, why put the people of this planet at risk? There are a thousand uninhabited worlds out there you could be using right now.'

'Overheads and logistics, primarily. A native population at a certain stage of technological development gave us ready access to locally sourced food supplies and an easily adaptable infrastructure, like this rather beautiful building.' A flicker of guilt momentarily crossed Febron's face before she continued: 'Along with a ready supply of live meat for our stock.'

'The thrill of the hunt improves the quality of the oil.' The Doctor recalled Henk's words. 'Homo sapiens. The gift that keeps on giving. I can't believe a biologist can have such disregard for an indigenous species.'

'We are all but links in the food chain, Doctor,' replied the scientist. 'Though I must admit, that aspect does not sit well with me. I would rather we let them hunt domesticated or wild mammals, but they seem to prefer sustenance from higher life forms. I suppose we should have expected as much.'

'Considering they've built up a small empire basically eating their way through the inhabitants of the planets they've invaded, I'd say that should have been the least you'd have expected.'

'Perhaps. But Mister Henk is quite correct, it does improve the purity of their glandular secretions. The oil, as you call it.'

'The oil that you're "farming".' The Doctor craned his neck, trying to get a clear view of the screens behind Febron, wondering where the oil was being siphoned off to. 'But what do you need it for? What possible use could it be to you?'

Febron smiled and casually flicked off the monitor. She got up and walked behind the Doctor, patting him on the shoulder as she passed by. 'You seem to be a clever boy. Work it out for yourself.'

With that, she unlocked the door leading up into the Cathedral, and spoke to a monk standing guard outside.

'I need to prepare myself for this evening. Watch the prisoner, and if he tries anything, or talks too much, use this.' She handed the guard a hypo and left.

The hooded monk watched her go, making sure she had disappeared from site before he closed and locked the door.

The Doctor gave him a cheerful wink. Looked like the strong silent type, he thought, which was good. He needed some peace and quiet to figure out what to do.

The monk took a step towards him and then, seeming to remember that the hood was all but covering his face, he reached up and pushed it back. 'Doctor,' he cried.

'Captain Darke. You clever old soldier.' The Doctor would happily have hugged the grizzled warrior, had he not been so effectively stuck to the chair. 'You couldn't untie me, could you? These ropes are beginning to chafe.'

The control centre was busy, fully manned and operational for the first time since its installation in one of the larger rooms leading off from the cloisters. There was a buzz of excitement about the place, nervous energy as the grand plan moved into a crucial phase.

Henk was deep in conversation with Branlo, standing near a flatbed monitor which showed a digital aerial representation of Worcester and the surrounding countryside. Coloured markers indicated the landing areas for five starships, each located at equidistant compass points, far enough from the city to avoid the attention of its inhabitants and each other. Smaller blinking blobs in matching colours indicated the current location of each ship's occupants.

'We've had a transmission from the Calabrian shuttle.' Branlo was reading from his datapad. 'They had some stability issues when they made planetfall. They want to recalibrate their flight control before leaving their ship, and send apologies for the delay to their arrival.'

Henk wasn't concerned at this development. 'I was wondering where they'd got to. It's not important. The Calabrians aren't major players anyway. They don't carry the same financial clout as some of our prospective customers. The Octulan delegation, for example – I'm expecting big things from them. Besides, all they'll miss will be the drinks and nibbles. What about the others?'

Branlo checked his list. 'The Octulan vessel has landed at its designated safe zone. They should be on their way here now. The Vrelt are still complaining about the density of Earth's atmosphere, and the X Imperative are making themselves at home in their quarters. Well, running a sensor sweep to make sure they aren't being bugged, but it seems to make them happy.'

'And the Siilutrax?'

'Should be here any second. I sent Gee out to meet them.'

'Excellent. Which leaves our late-running Calabrians.' Henk pondered. 'Let's hope they make it before nightfall. It would be embarrassing if they fell foul of our very own curfew. Perhaps I should instruct the Sheriff to lower the state of alert. I'm sure his troops would benefit from a night's rest.'

'Shall I run a final check on the presentation?'

'No, no. We've run through it often enough. I don't want my performance to seem over-rehearsed. Good work, Branlo. Carry on.'

As Henk made to leave, his attention was drawn to the security grid. A sudden urge took him to check on preparations in the Chapter House. Ignoring Archa, who sat sullenly at the terminal controls, doing his utmost to avoid being noticed by his boss, Henk reached in and switched security-cam views.

The Chapter House was the awe-inspiring venue for the evening's launch, and Henk had to admit that Earth's architects had a flair for grandiose simplicity. The cylindrical building contained just one large, round room, in which his people had constructed an impressive and sumptuous presentation space. At its centre, supporting the shallow conical roof, was a thick, tall pillar, surrounded at its base by a stage. Behind this, filling a substantial proportion of the room, was a glasscrete-fronted containment tank.

Henk smiled. If his guests weren't hooked in by his well-practised sales pitch, then the contents of that tank would have them reaching for their banker's drafts in no time.

NINE

Nothing moved in the silent woodland. Emily stared at the dead woman, whose body she'd discovered only minutes before but who was now apparently fully recovered and asking for help.

It had thrown Emily, still confused by the speed with which Henk's men had been killed, the ferocity of the attack. Why had she been spared?

The realisation immediately hit her that her situation had, if anything, just become a great deal more dangerous.

Emily blinked away the shock. 'Who are you?' she stammered. It was a lame question, but it was the only thought on her mind.

The Calabrian smiled gently, and bowed. 'I am Sister Toch'Lu of the Krillitane Horde, though you may be more familiar with the name that Henk's servile vagabonds saw fit to give me – Toeclaw.'

The Doctor had been right about the Krillitanes' ability to disguise their true forms. Emily looked at the calm, friendly woman before her, astonished that this could be the same brutish creature she'd glimpsed through her binocs, feeding on one of its victims. That memory was too potent to forget in a hurry. She would have to tread carefully. There was going to be no easy way out of this.

'Why would you need my help to kill Henk? From what I've seen, he wouldn't stand a chance against you.'

'When the time comes, his life will be mine the instant I choose to take it.' There was a hint of savagery behind the cultured tones of Toch'Lu, which was not lost on Emily. 'However,' the Krillitane continued, 'one needs to get close enough to one's prey before one can devour it, which is why I need you. Help me, and I shall ensure you do not come to any harm.'

Emily was well aware that she had no choice in the matter. She nodded. 'I'll help you. As it happens, I need to get back to the city, too. I have a friend there, so maybe we'll be able to help each other.'

Toch'Lu smiled, a smile as cold as the wintry mist clinging to the landscape around them, and offered a hand to Emily. She shook it, warily.

'Good. Good. Unfortunately we have little time. Follow me.'

Toch'Lu moved off, but Emily remained where she

was and nodded in the opposite direction. 'The city is that way. Where are you taking me?'

'Don't worry, I've eaten.' Toch'Lu stopped, flashing a demonic grin over her shoulder. 'First we must find a suitable disguise for you, which will gain us entry to Henk's stronghold as if we were welcome guests. By a stroke of good fortune I know the very place. The Calabrian ship is in this direction. There are uniforms aboard of which the crew no longer has any need.'

Emily watched as Toch'Lu continued on her way, obviously confident that the girl would follow her. Compared to the fate that had befallen her attackers, Emily realised she was doing well, for the time being at least. Still, it didn't make her feel any less uneasy about her current predicament.

They marched for a mile or so in silence, Emily keeping her distance from the Krillitane, watching for any sign of betrayal. Finally, they arrived in a cleared area of dense woodland which had obviously been prepared as a serviceable landing area for the Calabrian ship.

Toch'Lu had been honest about one thing – the crew really wouldn't be needing anything any more. A fresh pile of bones near the frigate's main hatch, which Emily did her best to ignore, suggested the Krillitane had already made herself a fine meal from the ship's crew.

'The crew's quarters are through there.' Toch'Lu pointed towards a cabin along the main access corridor. 'Apologies for the mess. One of the crew was particularly evasive.'

Emily stepped gingerly into the cabin, noting the smears of blood trailing across a bulkhead where some poor Calabrian had tried desperately to cling to life. She quickly changed into a close-fitting security guard's coverall. It was ideal: the uniform included a helmet with an opaque visor that would disguise her lack of forehead cartilage, such a prominent feature of the Calabrian race. This disguise was certainly more comfortable than the last one, she thought, adjusting a light but well-equipped Calabrian utility belt to sit better on her hips. She was ready. Checking that Toch'Lu couldn't see, Emily took her phase pistol from her parka and hid it beneath the armour padding of her new clothes, close enough to get to quickly if things turned nasty.

'It was fortuitous I came across you when I did.' The Krillitane's voice echoed through from the flight deck. 'Henk is no doubt expecting a delegation rather than an individual. Questions might have been asked.'

'Well, let's not keep him waiting,' replied Emily, grimly.

'That's the second time I've been tied up in less than twenty-four hours. Business as usual.' The Doctor stretched, glad to have full use of his limbs once again. 'Nice outfit. Where did you get it?'

Darke looked down at the cassock that disguised his armour. 'It belonged to our mystery visitor. The dead man we found last night. It is a bit bloodstained, but you can't really tell against the black cloth.'

'Wish I hadn't asked.'

'It served its purpose. I'm sorry I couldn't get here sooner, or I would've been able to warn you. At least they haven't killed you.'

'Always a bonus. How are things outside? Come to think of it, I don't even know what time it is.'

'Late afternoon, approaching dusk. There are a great many comings and goings.'

'Really?' asked the Doctor, thoughtfully. Both Henk and Febron had seemed preoccupied, excited even. 'I wonder if today's the big day?'

Sitting back down in the chair he'd vacated only moments before, the Doctor wheeled over to the computer terminal, sticking on his spectacles as he did so. With a flick of a switch, the screens glared brightly in the darkened room, and the Doctor leaned forward, fascinated. Now he had some idea of context, the myriad of data before him began to make perfect sense.

Darke, however, was almost overcome by the sudden glimpse of this technological devilry. Uncomfortable, he backed away. 'What is this, Doctor? These symbols that dance, this unnatural light... Such things are impossible.'

'Oh, the impossible is usually just a possible you hadn't thought of before. I knew someone once who tried to do twelve impossible things before breakfast. Always ended up burning his toast. Ah!' the Doctor exclaimed, enthusiastically.

'What? Are you hurt?' Darke stepped forward, hand

on the hilt of his sword, fully expecting the strange metal monster to leap into life and attack.

'No, no, it's fine.'

The Doctor pointed at the view he'd called up on one of the screens. One of Henk's monks was welcoming three tall, grey aliens in the nave. 'Those fellas there are Siilutrax, and unless they just happened to pop by for a cuppa, then they must be here to do business with the Bishop.'

Thoughtfully, the Doctor worked his way through various other cameras. No wonder Henk had been keen to keep him locked up and out of the way. The Cathedral was buzzing with activity.

'Interesting. They're pumping the Krillitane Oil out to a small plant in one of the buildings near the river. It's going into barrels. Easy to sell, barrels. But first it's going through some kind of distillation process.' He looked over at the sealed door leading into the crypt. 'In there.'

Darke followed his gaze. 'These Krillitanes are the horrors of which you spoke before? The monsters from beyond the stars?'

'Not really from beyond the stars as such, more various little bunches of stars they've plundered and called their own.'

'Then who are these people who have taken control of the Cathedral?'

'A different kind of monster. All too common. One fuelled by greed and avarice and profit. So the big question is, which monster do I deal with first, and how?'

The Doctor checked the data streams monitoring the life signs of the imprisoned Krillitanes, this time paying more attention to the finer details. 'Well, I suppose as we're here already, we might as well start with the Krillitanes. They're being fed on a perfectly balanced diet, a mixture of vitamins, proteins and animal fat, via nutrient tubes, but Febron is mixing in a constant flow of sedatives. If I alter the dose, then I should be able to revive one of them, get some answers.'

'Or we could slit their throats while they sleep.' Darke suggested, glancing sideways at the Doctor. 'Killing two birds with one stone. No more monsters.'

'In cold blood? Not my style, Captain. Not my style at all.' With that, the Doctor made his decision, reducing the flow of sedatives to the Krillitane that looked closest to consciousness. The same Krillitane that Febron had been tending to earlier.

'Prepare yourself, Captain. You're about to meet the Devil's Huntsman in person. All thirteen of them.'

The dreams folded in upon each other, a mess of sights and sounds, some memories, some imagined, but all so real.

The Brood Mother, falling away from him, always just out of reach, her head engulfed in flame, screaming, dying. Then the wide, fat visage of Henk, laughing in his face. Broken Wing lashed out, but his arms were no longer there, and Henk dissolved, mutating into Febron, holding some blunt metal object, pushing it into his body.

A roar of anger, mute in his chest. There was nothing he could do. Nothing.

And then there was the unmistakable sound of prey, the cautious footfalls, the scent of an easy kill.

Darke's sword was in his hand, his senses screaming at him to run, to get away from the nightmare beasts that hung in the half-light all around him. He gripped the hilt of his sword even tighter, ready to defend himself against inevitable attack. They walked slowly through the pillars, towards the alcove where one of the beasts was beginning to stir.

Broken Wing lifted his head at the sound of approaching footsteps, and the Doctor stopped instantly. The Krillitane blinked weakly at him, not yet fully conscious, but close to it. Close enough to be dangerous.

'Krillitane. We have a common enemy. The man that holds you and your brothers captive. Henk.'

The Krillitane let out a terrifying hiss at the name, back arched, striking out with his claws. After a moment it began to weaken, its arms falling back, limply.

'Are you sure about this, Doctor? This beast. It is the very Devil.' Darke whispered. He had lost any faith in a benevolent God many battles ago, but had never discounted the existence of the Lord's opposite number. He had never thought he might encounter the Devil face to face, however.

'Quite sure.' The Doctor stepped closer towards the

injured alien, examining a trail of wounds seared across its body, the scar betraying a surgical procedure having taken place at the nape of its neck. The Doctor carefully tested the area with his fingertips, feeling a solid lump that suggested an implant of some kind had been grafted to the Krillitane's cerebral cortex.

'They really have worked a number on you, haven't they?' he said softly, crouching down to make eye contact. 'What happened?'

An orange eye rolled from Darke to the Doctor, and Broken Wing spoke, his voice pained and cracked. 'What business is it of yours? This is a matter for the Brood. They killed her. They killed the Brood Mother, and we shall have our vengeance.' His voice cracked as his body convulsed into a fit of coughing, and he was visibly weaker when the spasms eventually subsided.

The Doctor glanced at the remote panel linked to Broken Claw's cell nearby, and expertly adjusted a few settings. 'I'm increasing the pain-relief dosage. It should help. I met your Brood Mother, and she was very much alive. There's a good chance she still could be.'

Broken Claw could already feel the agony of his wounds easing. The hated blue scientist, Febron, had administered only a minimum dosage, and it had made little difference.

'She's dead. We each have a neural inhibitor implant. If she had escaped, Henk would have sent a remote signal, an electrical bolt causing total neural meltdown. She could not have survived.'

That explained the device he'd found beside the body in the alley, thought the Doctor. A control box allowing a handler to punish his charge with various degrees of pain via the implant, if it threatened to misbehave. Of course Henk would have had a long-range, failsafe back-up, just in case.

'But how did your Brood end up here? Krillitane aren't exactly pushovers. How did Henk capture you?'

'Why should I tell you?' Broken Wing spat back. 'You are just another humanoid, no doubt in league with Henk.'

'If I was, surely I'd already know?'

'Doctor, you speak with the monster as if in conversation, but the beast replies with the growls of an animal. How do you understand it?' Darke asked, perplexed.

'Long story, but he can understand every word you say, so mind your Ps and Qs.' The Doctor turned back to Broken Wing, who was studying the Doctor slyly.

'Your animal smells of sweat and fear, surely an indigenous creature. A primitive. But you? Your scent is not familiar. What are you?'

'Oh, nothing much, in the grand scheme of things. Just a passer-by. Tell me what happened. I can help.'

Broken Wing considered his situation. He could feel his strength returning, and soon he would be able to break free of his bonds. He could kill this puny biped then, if he so chose, but perhaps there might be some advantage in keeping the Doctor alive. His obvious medical skills could be useful in reviving the rest of the Brood. Yes, he would tell the Doctor his story. There was no shame in it.

'The journey is not important. We were fugitives, forced to flee our homeworld along with our Brood. We travelled to a region of the galaxy where the Krillitane are unknown, where we could stay hidden from our enemies, and settled on a densely populated planet, rich with meat and the opportunity to hunt. But one of our young fell ill.'

'Someone she ate? Sorry. Bad taste.' The Doctor winced. 'Sorry. Ignore me. Carry on.'

Broken Wing waited for any more foolish interruptions before continuing. 'Under normal circumstances, the weakling would have been excluded from the Brood, but we were already of limited number and the loss of a future warrior was not an option. That was when we encountered the blue scientist, Belinna Febron.'

The Doctor raised his eyebrows. 'I bet she couldn't believe her luck. A brand new, unknown alien life form, walking right in through her front door.'

'She had a good reputation, and we were desperate,' Broken Wing told him. 'We took the form of her race and made contact with her. She is a skilled biologist and saved the youngling, but in the process she learnt enough of our physiology to become a threat. I should have killed her then. What we didn't know was that she had entered into partnership with a business associate in order to fund her own research. Soon after, she and Henk arrived at our hiding place while we slept, armed with tranquilliser guns and manpower. Since then we have been prisoners. No, worse, nothing more than cattle, to be experimented upon.' Broken Wing shuddered and hissed through his fangs.

'Funny you should mention cattle, cos in a way that's what they're using you for. A herd of cattle.' The Doctor rocked on his heels, still crouching to maintain eye contact with the Krillitane. 'They're milking you. Well, oiling, I suppose you'd call it. Taking your oil and filtering it and draining it into barrels. Why would they be doing that, do you think?'

Broken Wing didn't answer for a moment. He could feel the cold hypersteel tubes that penetrated the skin painfully beneath his jaw, stabbing into two small glands which produced the very fluid that made the Krillitane what they were. A unique species in all the universe. 'The Oil is our essence, Doctor. The source of our greatest achievements. It gives us the power to evolve on our own terms, to adapt and to survive, to fashion ourselves into the ultimate life form. Yet while it enables us to do great things, it has damned our race to its core.'

'You call the slaughter of the entire Bessan civilisation a great achievement? No wonder your own bodies are trying to poison you.'

The Krillitane's eyes narrowed. 'You know of my race?'

'Yeah, and to be honest I'd usually have no sympathy for you, but today you got lucky. I need to get you off this planet, before you decide to pilfer its infinite biological diversity and mash it up into whatever you decide looks pretty next.' The Doctor made another adjustment to the life-support systems, then stood up and began to walk away. 'But I promise you, I will do my best to get you out of here. All of you.'

'Where are you going?' the Krillitane hissed, irritated by the Doctor's impudence. 'If Henk is your enemy, then we are friends. Release me, and we can join forces against him.'

The Doctor stopped beside Darke, who had been hanging back for most of the bizarre, seemingly one-sided exchange. 'The moment I set you free, I become a free lunch, and there's no such thing. You can stay up there for now, until I figure out what to do with you. I'll be back.'

Broken Wing stared after the pair as they disappeared into the shadows in silence. As a wave of impotent anger grew within him, he recognised the cloudy sensation of sedation clawing at his consciousness. His lip curled as he committed the Doctor's scent to memory. There would be a reckoning.

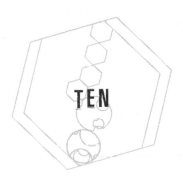

TEN

'Mind how you go, Sam,' John Garrud cried warmly after the old man, his best customer, staggering away through the snow.

Old Samuel was always the last to leave, and tonight was no exception. Silly old fool always managed to get home in one piece, whatever state he was in. The Huntsman would've taken one sniff of the inebriated gent and left him well enough alone.

John sighed, and stared up at the dark sky. Not even a glimpse of the setting sun tonight, only thick clouds, threatening another snowstorm. After all the fuss and terror of the previous night, a heavy snowfall didn't hold the same sense of foreboding as it used to.

He was about to shut and bolt the door when he heard hurried footsteps crunching on the snow further along the street. Too early for the first patrol, thought the innkeeper. He held the door open, just a crack, enough to have a bit of a nose at whoever was about to pass by, and pressed his eye against the crack, waiting for them to come into view. So long as it wasn't another stranger like that Doctor fellow. He'd been pleasant enough company, but the last thing they needed was for their inn to get a reputation for harbouring murderous scoundrels and miscreants, however well mannered.

A few moments later and there they were, two figures, soldiers possibly, clad in unusual orange armour. One of them had the bearing of aristocracy, a hooded cloak billowing in the wind behind her. The other, walking at a measured distance behind, was obviously a bodyguard, albeit slight in stature.

As they passed, the lead figure suddenly glared directly towards John's hiding place, and inclined her head in a bow. There was no way she could have seen him, and her smile chilled his bones to the marrow.

Alarmed, John shut the door and slammed the bolt home, leaning against it for good measure.

Best not mention that to the wife, he decided.

Henk took a sip from his glass and watched the assorted new arrivals warily interact or avoid contact altogether, and fleetingly worried that a meet-and-greet function before the main show might have been a mistake.

The atmosphere in the Rectory was uncomfortable to say the least. Amongst the delegates, at least two groups had a history of inter-species conflict, though Henk had known that already, and was counting on their antipathy influencing the course of negotiations. That none of them knew the precise nature of Henk's product was also causing hackles to be raised to match their expectations.

He had brought together this disparate group very particularly, carefully selected to ensure that he had something to offer each and every one of them, a product that would fulfil any number of very unique requirements, and that some would be desperate to obtain if they saw their historic enemies doing so. Maximum profitability was his primary concern.

A quiet cough from behind snapped him out of his reverie. It was Branlo.

'Sir, the Calabrian delegate and her escort have just arrived,' the lad whispered discreetly, not wishing to spend any more time amongst these business people than he had to. These alien races freaked him out.

'About time. Hurry them along, Branlo. The others are becoming restless. I think it's time to kick off the main event.'

Henk noticed Belima, nervously clutching a glass of some herbal infusion and avoiding eye contact with anyone that threatened to pass too close. He wandered over to her.

'You look radiant.' He smiled, meaning it. He usually went for blondes, but blue was equally appealing. Perhaps, when all this was over, they could get to know each other better while watching the profits roll in. 'Don't worry, I won't make you talk to any of them in person.'

'Good job. It's bad enough my work has to be reduced to a commodity in order for it to reach its fullest potential.' Febron gazed into her glass, as if looking for answers. She'd known where things were going when she'd first signed on with Henk, and it was pointless bemoaning the depths one had to sink to simply to secure funding. Her work was more important.

'After tonight, everything you've striven for, all your sacrifices will have been worth it. And the universities and corporations that shied away from the moral ambiguities of what you have achieved will regret their lack of vision.' Henk laid a reassuring hand on her shoulder. 'The final delegate has arrived, so we can begin.'

The Doctor's eyes sparkled, staring into a small glass vial suspended amongst an intricate web of electronics and filtering equipment, where a dense yellow fluid gathered slowly, dripping from the nozzle of a brass tube. 'She's brilliant. Quite brilliant,' he muttered, as another tiny drip plopped silently into the vial.

'All the Krillitanes seem to do is sleep and eat,' Darke muttered, paying little attention to the contraption that so entranced the Doctor. Instead, he nervously watched the far end of the crypt for any sign that the winged creature had slipped its bonds. 'Your collection of bottles and pipes may be fascinating, but I'm more concerned that the beast will only sleep for so long, before indulging in its other favourite pastime.'

'No need to worry about him,' the Doctor said absently, concentrating on unclipping the vial of precious fluid and carefully lifting it out of the spaghetti-like mess of technology. 'I made sure he'll get a full night's sleep. He won't be bothering anyone for a while. Probably have a bit of a head on him when he wakes up, though.'

Decanting the viscous fluid into a test tube he'd retrieved from his jacket pocket, the Doctor squeezed a rubber stopper in the end, before pushing the now empty vial back into its resting place with a click. 'That'll set them back a bit I should think. Right. Come on.' The Doctor leapt to his feet and ran off in the direction of the anteroom.

Darke took another look into the shadows before hurrying after him. He was happier once they were on the other side of the reinforced security door, trapping the monsters on the other side.

The Doctor was already sitting at the monitoring station, chattering away excitedly. 'The thing about the Krillitanes, the really amazing thing about them, is that they don't have to wait for thousands of generations to evolve. If they find a weakness in their physiology, they can change it. All they need to do is find another species with the attribute they need, and they take it. Bang. Next generation, problem solved. A species that truly controls its own destiny.'

Darke shrugged. There was a reason he'd chosen soldiering over a career as an apothecary.

Recognising the blank stare of incomprehension on the

soldier's face, the Doctor remembered that the universal truths of the twelfth century were very different to those of the human race post-Darwin. Well, most of them.

'Sorry, I'm racing ahead a bit. Missed out the Reformation and the Renaissance entirely, but they're not really your problem. All you need to understand is that the Krillitanes have the power to take the essence of any living creature they choose, and make it part of themselves.'

'You make them sound like gods. Vengeful gods.' Darke glanced at the security door, not so sure that mere metal could hold back such powerful beings.

'Oh, not so much "vengeful". Not even malicious really. As far as they're concerned, it's their birthright. They've leapfrogged their way up the food chain, quicker than their culture could mature. Super-intelligent, hyper-evolved geniuses, but with the mentality of pack animals, governed by their primal urge to hunt. More like a gang of selfish, greedy children with unrestricted access to a sweet shop.'

The Doctor sniffed. 'Anyway, everything the Krillitanes are, everything they do, is the result of an evolutionary quirk of fate, an insignificant hiccup in the grand scheme of things. Just a few thousand years ago, a tiny gland that controlled their ancestors' ageing process started producing a brand new chemical.' He jiggled the test tube of oil extract, a look of wonder on his face. 'Never seen before in all of time and space, and suddenly they became unique in the universe. Only, as vital as the oil is to them, it's also lethal. A blessing and a curse. Safe enough when it's tucked up inside their glands, but poison upon contact with their skin. They have to drain themselves every day. Very carefully.'

'No wonder they are so angry. So it is this oil that gives them their power?'

'Absolutely. Sort of. This enzyme usually stays mixed in with all the other chemicals in the oil. The Krillitanes have never thought to separate it, why would they? But Belima Febron not only identified it from a chance encounter, she's managed to isolate the specific chemical and filter it out into a quantifiable commodity, and that's what this is all about.'

The Doctor paused, deeply impressed by the contents of the thin glass tube he held between his fingers.

'She's bottled evolution.'

Emily glanced up towards the vaulted ceiling of the nave, looking for likely escape routes. With wings like the Krillitanes', she might have stood a chance of making it to the windows, but they were too high to be any kind of option for her. The only other exit led deeper into the Cathedral, and yet again she regretted not taking more care in getting to know the lay of the land. It wasn't as if you could fail to notice this edifice of white stone.

She would have to stick with Toch'Lu for a while yet and hope that by chance she might stumble across the Doctor if, as she suspected, he had already found his own way in here.

Toch'Lu was talking to the awkward young man who had come to welcome them. 'I can only apologise for the lateness of our arrival,' Toch'Lu explained smoothly to him. 'The repairs our vessel needed were rather more extensive than at first thought. I do hope we haven't missed anything important.'

'Not at all, Baroness Deel. In fact, you couldn't have timed your arrival better. We're about to begin, so if you'd care to follow me?' Branlo felt more comfortable with the Calabrians, humanoids like him rather than the exotic beings he'd been looking after for the past few hours.

'Of course.' Toch'Lu bowed, and they followed Branlo through into the cloisters, just in time to see the last of the delegates trailing into the Chapter House. Emily recognised the tentacled robotic travelpod of an Octulan as it disappeared through the doors.

A moment later and they had crossed the threshold into a huge circular room, where each of the delegates was being ushered into comfortably appointed areas, designed specifically for their individual needs. Emily noted that each was fitted with an induction loop patched into a universal language translator. The attention to detail was impressive. Henk had either spared no expense or, more likely, used his extensive criminal contacts to get all this stuff.

Toch'Lu and Emily were shown to the Calabrian seating area, richly carpeted and furnished with a collection of genuine and reproduction Calabrian antiques. Emily took a seat behind her Krillitane companion, where she could keep an eye out for trouble.

The Octulans were a few delegations away, past the Siilutrax and a group of tall, grey aliens she couldn't identify. There were three Octulans, their travelpods now docked with a pressurised communal bubble that dominated their area, into which each pink mass of flesh had shuffled. Earth's atmosphere was too dense for them to exist outside of their protective travelpods, but as a species they delighted in physical contact, so the clever inclusion of an enclosure was another Henk masterstroke.

Henk. The thought of the man made her shudder. This had not been supposed to happen, and she'd tried so desperately hard to avoid it. Emily took a deep breath to steady her nerves.

All around her, the hum of conversation was beginning to die away into expectant silence. Something was about to happen. All eyes turned towards a raised platform that stood before an onyx-like curve of glass that filled a sizeable area of the space.

The lights dimmed.

'Imagine,' echoed a deep voice from hidden speakers, making Emily jump. 'Imagine, if you will, being handed the keys to your God's celestial palaces. Gifted their powers and infinite wisdom. Given free rein to enact your vision of a perfect universe. Ask yourself. What would be your first act?'

With a rolling scale of notes, electronic music

now filled the air, and a video presentation began, shimmering into life upon the bulky onyx wall beside the stage. Images of suns being born, planets forming from lumps of rock and dust, the crucible of molten lava and chemical compounds as the images zoomed in to microscopic levels, to watch the first simple, single-cell bacteria seemingly spring out of nowhere. The images began to speed up, as multi-celled organisms developed into aquatic creatures, transforming into stump-limbed things that flopped out of the seas and onto wet sand…

And all the while a clock at the foot of the screen sped at an insane rate through the millennia.

'The story of life is the same across the galaxies, enshrined in myth and legend, explored through science, revered by religion, but the power to take hold of life, to transform and improve it, has never rested in the hands of mortal beings. Until now.'

The music, which culminated in a rousing crescendo, faded to a sonorous background hum, while a complicated chemical equation replaced video footage, scrolling across the screen as if being handwritten by a fevered, invisible ghost.

'Good evening. Tonight we are presenting to you a breakthrough in genetic science that has the potential to change the course of history,' said the same voice that had accompanied the presentation, only this time it wasn't a recording.

Emily dug her fingernails into the finely turned wooden arms of her chair, knuckles whitening, and she gritted her teeth as a spotlight picked out the figure of a large, imperious-looking man who had taken position on the stage while the audience's attention had been enraptured by the somewhat over-the-top presentation.

It was him. It was Henk, and hatred exploded in Emily's heart.

The security monitor had been scrolling through different cameras automatically, before holding on a shot looking down on the gathering in the Chapter House. A montage of images played out on a screen in front of the assembled guests.

'Ooh, look, they've started. I wonder if we can get sound on this thing?' He reset a few audio parameters and music blasted into the small antechamber. Darke clamped his hands against his ears and the Doctor hastily turned the volume down. 'Sorry.'

'… Until now.' An echoing voice crackled through the tinny speakers, which the Doctor recognised as Henk's. No sign of him in person, though, as the camera remained focused on the screen that was now covered in words, rendered illegible by the resolution of the monitoring station. The Doctor squinted, trying to make some sense of them, but the camera suddenly whipped away, stopping on an image of Henk himself, bathed in the glow of a spotlight. Oddly he looked more trustworthy now he'd ditched the Bishop's garb and was wearing an expensive-looking and very fashionably cut suit.

'That's our man, Captain.'

'Good evening.' The little grey image of Henk continued. 'Tonight we are presenting to you a breakthrough in genetic science that has the potential to change the course of history.'

The Doctor groaned. 'Here we go. Typical salesman, trotting out empty patter left, right and centre. You can't "change" history. It's already happened. You can influence your own future, but you can't change everybody's past. Well, you can, but you're not supposed to. It gets so messy and… Hang on, where are we off to now?' The camera was on the move again, panning down and to the left, finally holding and zooming in on a delegation whose number seemed to be rather depleted, given the handful of empty chairs in their area.

'I don't think much of the director. What kind of audience reaction shot is that? You can't even see their faces,' complained the Doctor.

Darke was looking closely at the screen, thinking. 'Why would this spy in a box seek out these people, amongst all the others? It is as if they are of special interest, though to me they look no less normal than you or I.'

'That is a very good point, Captain. Someone in security has singled them out. They must be scanning them, but why now? Surely Henk's people would have run thorough checks on all the delegates as soon as they arrived. Unless they arrived fashionably late…' The Doctor rubbed his chin, unwelcome thoughts percolating at the back of his mind. 'I need to access the full security grid. Should be able to do it from here.'

The Doctor's fingers were a blur of motion on the keyboard, until a new data panel opened on the screen, containing the same security camera shot but with a panoply of additional data. 'Aha. I love integrated computer networks. Such a doddle to potter about in. Oh. Oh, this isn't good.' The Doctor's face fell, and he checked the data again. 'This is in no way good.'

'What is it, Doctor? What do you see?' Darke peered at the monitor, unable to understand the readings that had so disheartened his companion.

'No wonder security is interested,' whispered the Doctor. 'That delegate isn't who she's supposed to be.'

ELEVEN

Emily could feel the lump of her phase pistol, hidden inside her uniform. It would be so easy to take Henk down right now, just draw the weapon and fire. Now she was here, why not? The bounty had been paid, or at least enough of it to cover her costs. And it wasn't about the money anyway. Henk was right there, a sitting target, hers for the taking, yet common sense held her back. It wasn't the right time. Security was discreet but heavy, and they would be on her the moment she reached inside her tunic.

Clenching her teeth, she resolved to wait. Their luck had held this far, so there was no reason to believe a better opportunity wouldn't present itself.

Despite her focus on Henk, Emily realised she hadn't been listening to a word he'd been saying, and curiosity began to get the better of her. Until now she'd had no interest in Henk's reasons for being on this planet, just that he was. Even having spent time with the Doctor, and meeting Toch'Lu, she'd not given a thought to what linked him with the Krillitanes. Right now there was nothing she could do but listen, and she had to admit that Henk was certainly an impressive orator, a master at engaging with a large audience as if his words were directed at each individual alone.

'Many of you have travelled halfway across this galaxy to be here, following intricate routes which I have insisted upon to maintain the exclusive nature of this event. Each of you has taken an interest in what I have to offer, yet thus far I have offered only the merest micron of detail, a scratch upon the surface of possibility, just enough to pique your interest into making the arduous journeys you have all endured.' Henk looked humble. 'And for this I apologise. Now all shall be revealed, and you will understand my reasons for such circumspection.'

Behind Henk, the giant onyx screen was beginning to clear, pixel by pixel, a harsh yellow light bursting through the tiny gaps which grew in number and began to merge, like a disease spreading across a Petri dish. Henk continued to speak while the light's intensity increased, a supernova exploding over his shoulder.

'I asked you to imagine what you would do with the power of a god. I can think of nothing more powerful than the ability to protect your own species, to ensure that it survives and prospers in the battle to thrive in this harsh universe.' Henk, delighted by his own showmanship, had a warm glow in his stomach. 'Thanks to the astonishing work of the galaxy's pre-eminent biologist, we have made this dream a reality. For a negotiable fee, payable in instalments over a fixed licence period, we can give you that power.'

The onyx screen was now entirely translucent, revealing an interior that resembled a holding pen. At the rear of the pen was a row of arc lamps, the source of the startling yellow light which now filled the Chapter House, and Emily was grateful for the polarised visor on her Calabrian helmet.

She could see a shape moving inside, silhouetted against the lights, familiar yet new, moving into plain view as if following a well-rehearsed and choreographed routine. A huge, angular living thing, light reflecting from armoured shoulders, four muscular legs supporting a torso covered by a protective carapace. From its back stretched long wings, filling the width of the holding pen. Larger than Toch'Lu by far, the creature was unmistakably of Krillitane descent, yet composed of striking physical elements appropriated from any number of other species. A showroom model with all the extras, created solely to make an instant and unforgettable impression on its audience.

'During a scientific expedition to a primitive planet in the Omarra sector, Doctor Belima Febron discovered a previously unknown species,' Henk continued. 'The Krillitanes. A species that naturally generates a malleable genome, that can be harnessed and recoded using our proprietary technology. We can bio-engineer this species into forms that fit your specific needs, whether all you require is a passive, tireless agricultural drone, or a sentient mining machine immune to high-level croprastic bombardment, or perhaps a savage weapon that will follow your orders into any environment, and carry them out to the death. This is the power we give to you. Behold – the Krillitane Storm,' Henk declared with triumph.

As if on cue, his creation bared its teeth and roared. One by one the audience got to their feet, those that had them, and a round of applause swept across the room, a wave of appreciation, greedy eyes already planning new empires using this wonderful toy.

There was one notable exception, however: the Calabrian delegation remained silent amid the excitement.

Toch'Lu made a move towards the stage, but Emily clasped a restraining hand on her shoulder. 'Don't,' she implored, knowing it was no use.

Toch'Lu twisted free, and turned on Emily. 'Do not presume to command me. In gratitude for assisting me this far, I advise you to leave here. Now. Henk, and his assembly of scavengers, must pay for his lies. For this abomination.'

'You don't stand a chance, Toch'Lu.' Emily stared, pleading, into Toch'Lu's eyes but saw only blind rage. She glanced around the room. Security had already taken an interest in them. Then she caught a glimpse of the young man that had welcomed them, whispering something in Henk's ear. Henk, aghast, stared straight at them. Their cover was blown. Emily looked back at Toch'Lu. 'They'll kill you.'

'My life is unimportant. Beneath this temple my brethren, my children, are held prisoner. Release them for me, and if I fall, they will avenge my death.' Toch'Lu pulled away, and before Emily's shocked eyes, returned to her true form.

The image of the Calabrian ambassador dissolved into a dust storm, swirling, twisting, expanding, re-coalescing into the brutal, hungry shape of a Krillitane. Toch'Lu swung her face towards Henk, pulling back her lips to reveal razor-sharp fangs, and she let loose a dreadful, vicious howl.

In the antechamber, the Doctor leapt out of his chair. On the screen, the other Calabrian, the one that hadn't transformed into an alien killing machine, had just thrown aside her helmet, revealing a shock of unmistakable, short blonde hair. 'No. No, that's Emily,' the Doctor exclaimed, gesticulating at the screen. 'I knew she'd end up in trouble. Come on, Captain. And bring your sword.'

There was a moment of shocked silence, as the delegates wondered if this was all part of the show. Toch'Lu roared again and leapt forward, half-sprinting, half-flying directly towards Henk, slashing wildly at anyone unfortunate enough to cross her path.

The room erupted into full-blown panic. Monks were running towards Toch'Lu, drawing blasters from the folds of their robes, but a few had their sights set firmly on Emily.

'That's that, then,' she whispered and, without looking back, took full advantage of the sudden confusion and dived into the throng that was flooding towards the only exit.

Toch'Lu sprang at Henk, claws outstretched, ready to rip him apart. Henk watched, unmoving, unconcerned, and too late Toch'Lu recognised her mistake. She smashed into the invisible protective force wall that Henk had installed at the edge of the stage. Sparks of energy flitted across her body, and she collapsed, unconscious, to the floor.

Unaware of Toch'Lu's fate, though suspecting it would be terminal, Emily fought her way through the mangle of desperate bodies, and all but fell through the door into the cloisters.

'You. Stop where you are, or we'll shoot,' a voice shouted from the left. More monks with guns.

Wasting no time, she was on the run, heading right, towards the nave. With luck, she might even make the main door. Limestone shattered under a hail of gunfire above her head, but Emily didn't stop. She leapt up a set of stone steps and flew through the doors so fast she didn't have time to avoid crashing into some fool running in the opposite direction.

'Get out of my—'

Strong hands gripped her, and she looked up into a familiar face. 'Emily, it's me. It's the Doctor.'

'God, I could kiss you.'

'Yeah, I get that a lot. No time right now. This way.'

The Doctor pulled Emily to one side, as a pair of Henk's monks bowled through the doorway and straight into the path of Captain Darke's fists. The first crashed to the floor, unconscious, but the other recovered enough to swing his gun towards the Doctor. Darke's sword smashed the guards weapon from his hand, and a well-placed boot sent the assailant tumbling backwards through the open door. The Captain slammed it shut before the guard could gather his wits, and braced himself against the pressure of bodies soon hammering against the other side.

'Doctor. The brace.' Darke nodded at a hefty wooden bar, propped against the door frame.

The Doctor strained to lift it, slamming the brace into its iron brackets. 'Not exactly Fort Knox, but it should hold them off for a bit.'

And the three of them were running again, across the marble floor, away from the muffled fury emanating from the cloisters.

'I thought you'd gone,' the Doctor panted, glancing at Emily.

'I did, but I had to come back, to warn you.'

'About what? That you're best mates with a Krillitane?'

'No. She saved my life. I had to help her. It's not as if she gave me a choice.'

Ahead of them the main doors burst open, and half a dozen monks charged in. Grabbing Emily's hand, the Doctor dragged her to the right, shouting through gritted teeth, 'Change of plan.'

'Run, Doctor. I shall hold them,' shouted Darke, brandishing his sword and ploughing into the surprised men with a hearty battle cry.

The Doctor and Emily sped towards the other end of the Cathedral, desperately searching for another way out, or at least a decent hiding hole. The crypt was no good, and they were about to run out of options.

'Why don't they build more exits in these places? Haven't they ever heard of emergencies?' the Doctor complained.

'There,' Emily shouted, pointing towards an alcove beyond which a staircase spiralled upwards, presumably to the top of the tower.

They sprinted towards the alcove but had only made it up a few steps when they were confronted by yet another monk on his way down. With a look of shock on his face he raised his energy rifle and fired, but the fugitives had already turned tail and skidded back into the Cathedral.

More monks were heading towards them from the nave, carrying an assortment of blasters and disruptor rifles. Darke's rearguard action must have failed. It was becoming clear there wasn't going to be any way out of this.

'You may as well save your energy, Doctor. You are completely surrounded, and your little soldier boy has been disarmed.' Henk's voice echoed across the vast chamber, as he walked calmly towards them, Branlo at his side.

Just behind them, the unconscious Darke was being half-carried, half-dragged by a couple of monks. They dumped him unceremoniously to the floor.

'As for you, dear girl,' said Henk, 'what is your story, I wonder? You're not a Calabrian, that's for sure. Your nose is far too pretty. Well, we'll have plenty of time to find out later. Guards, restrain them.'

'Not again,' groaned the Doctor, as his arms were grabbed and pulled behind his back.

Another of the monks reached for Emily but, before he could get a firm grip on her, she'd dropped to one knee, twisting and firing her phase pistol blindly. Pain exploded in the monk's thigh, a flesh wound but enough to send him tumbling to the floor with a shrill squeak.

Emily was back on her feet in an instant, walking purposefully towards Henk, her outstretched arm aiming her pistol squarely at his chest.

The Doctor strained against his captors. He had to stop Emily from doing something stupid. 'Emily, drop the gun. Whatever it is he did to you, killing him won't put it right. Think about what you're doing.'

'Hold your fire, lads, I think the young lady has

something to say.' Henk smirked, winking at the Doctor. 'I like this one. Feisty.'

Emily stopped, a couple of metres from Henk. Too late to change her mind now, whatever the Doctor said. Just pull the trigger. Nothing else mattered.

'So what's this all about, then? Finishing the job for your friend, Toeclaw?' taunted Henk. 'Well? Come on, little girl, say your piece. Nice shot, by the way, but you're no professional.' It was as if the threat of assassination were as much of an inconvenience as choosing what to have for lunch. 'No, this is personal, isn't it?'

Emily bit her lip, felt tiny beads of sweat forming along her hairline, her heart pounding. One shot. That was all it would take.

'Mister Branlo here tells me you're of Ertrari origin. Oh, I should mention we took a full bio-scan when we ran a belated security sweep on you earlier.' Henk referred to a datapad he was carrying, and smiled apologetically. 'Due to a scheduling oversight we didn't have an opportunity to do so upon your arrival, or we would have been able to avoid all this tiresome running around.'

He put a finger to his lips, as if pondering some matter that weighed upon his mind. 'If memory serves, I had some dealings with an Ertrari bounty hunter a month or so ago. Isn't that a coincidence?'

Emily stared coldly at the smug monster before her. 'You killed him,' she spat, trembling with anger.

'No, not at all.' Handing the pad back to Branlo, Henk took a few nonchalant steps towards Emily. 'I *had* him killed, yes, but I wouldn't dirty my hands with that kind of business. I did, however, torture him first. Not that I expected to gain any useful information from him, you understand. It's just a hobby of mine.'

Tears were welling up in Emily's eyes. Trying to blink them away, breathing hard, she sobbed, 'You killed him. You killed my daddy, and now I'm going to kill you.'

'Oh, I don't think so. Granted, you were brave to come here, to think you could pull it off. Brave, but not a killer. Unlike your father, though he wasn't a very good one. I certainly wouldn't have hired him. Still, his visit wasn't completely wasted. Once I'd finished having my fun, he made a rather pleasant between-meals snack for the Krillitane. I don't imagine Toeclaw brought that up in conversation, did she? Probably still picking the bits from between her teeth.'

'You...' Emily squeezed the trigger, but she wasn't quick enough. Henk swung out with his left arm, grabbing her wrist and yanking it painfully upwards and to the side, the weapon discharging harmlessly towards the ceiling. Then he struck a vicious blow across Emily's cheek, with such force that it lifted the girl from her feet and sent her sprawling across the cold, hard floor.

The Doctor wrenched himself free and rushed over to her, cradling the weeping girl in his arms. 'It's all right. It's all right,' he whispered, holding her tightly. He looked angrily up at Henk, eyes blazing. 'That wasn't necessary.'

'I've been working on this project for too long to see it go down the pan now thanks to some treacherous livestock and a whining child. Don't worry, she won't be alive long enough to feel the bruise. None of you will,' Henk sneered at the Doctor. 'Now if you'll excuse me, I have something of a damage-limitation exercise on my hands.'

Some order had been restored to the Chapter House. Although shocking, Toch'Lu's assault on the stage had been so short-lived that the panic had subsided almost as quickly as it had begun. Those few delegates who had attempted to flee were either engaged in face-saving conversations with their companions, whom they had left to fend for themselves, or keeping a low profile.

It had taken several of Henk's burlier employees to drag the battered Krillitane into the cloisters, and out of sight. Febron bent over the creature, carrying out a brief medical examination to assess if the force wall had done any permanent damage. She winced at the deep wound where the Krillitane had torn out her implant, although amazingly it was already well on the way to being fully healed, suggesting advanced molecular reconstruction. Was there no end to the potential benefits to medical science that were inherent to the Krillitanes?

'You are one resilient female,' Febron observed, impressed at the staying power of the species, especially this individual.

'Personally, I wish she'd stayed dead,' an impatient voice grumbled behind her. 'At least we know where *her* daughters are.' Henk had returned, and he wasn't happy. This girl turning up to avenge her father's death was irritation enough, but he'd never discovered who had hired the bounty hunter in the first place, and this worrying thought had festered at the back of his mind ever since.

Febron clipped a collar around Toch'Lu's neck, and tapped a code into the control pad on its rear panel. Standing back, she watched as the Krillitane form shifted, becoming the Calabrian Ambassador once more. 'The collar excites the neural pathways that control her morphic ability. At least she'll be easier to manage like this. Did you catch the other one?'

Henk nodded. 'Along with your playmate the Doctor, and some random thug with a sword. One of the Doctor's associates, I should think. Must've been the one who let him out of the crypt. For want of a decent cell, I've had them locked up in a room at the west end of the cloisters. Might as well throw Toeclaw in there, too. Once I've reassured our guests that we're not complete amateurs, I intend to have the Doctor and his friends executed.'

TWELVE

In a spot of nothingness halfway between the orbits of Saturn and Jupiter, a starship blinked out of hyperspace.

The ship was ugly, functional and heavily armed. It continued along the same trajectory upon which it had arrived, heading directly towards the sun, a bright pinprick against the oily blackness. Then it changed tack, swinging its blunt nose around on a new bearing. Sub-light engines powering up, the vessel surged forwards, increasing speed towards its target destination. Earth.

The Doctor shone a penlight into Captain Darke's eyes. The soldier had taken a nasty blow to the head, but there didn't seem to be any lasting damage.

'I held them back as long as I could, Doctor, but there

were just too many of them. I'm not as young as I was.'

'You're not the only one. You'll have a nasty bump for a bit, but you'll live,' the Doctor reassured the still-dazed Captain.

Darke looked over at Emily. She sat alone at the far end of the room, staring at the disguised Krillitane who had been dumped, unconscious, nearby. 'What about the girl?'

'I don't know, Captain.' The Doctor sighed. Time for a long overdue chat, he decided, and wandered over, sitting himself down beside the dejected young woman.

'One day, they'll probably turn this into a little shop.' he said, conversationally. 'Guide books, cuddly bears, little silver spoons with national flags on the handles, that kind of thing.'

Emily remained silent. Perhaps a more direct approach was needed. 'Why didn't you tell me what you were doing here?'

She sniffed, and wiped at her nose with a crumpled cloth she'd been using to soak up her tears. 'I didn't know you. How could I trust you? For all I knew, you could have been working for Henk. You might even have been him.'

'Seventeenth rule of survival: Trust No One. Mulder's Law, they call it. Not a big fan, myself, but then I do end up in more than my fair share of scrapes, so maybe there's something in it.' A hint of a smile on Emily's lips satisfied the Doctor that he hadn't lost her completely, and he smiled back, warmly.

'So, what happened?' he asked.

Thinking about her father was something she'd been avoiding, the shock of his death too recent, too painful to face. Emily sighed.

'My dad was a bounty hunter, small-scale, nothing dangerous. Usually tracking bail jumpers for a couple of agencies he freelanced for. It was a living. Anyway, a job came along that offered amazing rates, enough to cover my university fees for a couple of years, too good to miss, so off he went.

'Then his signal went dead. It was an insurance thing, a bio-link between Dad and his ship. If something…' The grief threatened to overwhelm her again, but she fought it back. 'If something happened to him, the ship would transmit an emergency call to base.' Emily closed her eyes, remembering the moment she'd heard the terrible news.

Over the course of his nine hundred-odd years, the Doctor had seen many friends come and go, and each had left an indelible mark upon him. He knew well enough how hard it was to lose someone you loved. 'I'm sorry,' he sympathised.

'I've known the people at the Agency all my life,' Emily continued, feeling better for talking. 'Since we lost Mum, they've been like family, and they contacted me straight away. I had to know what had happened, so I dropped out of college and told them I'd take on the job, track down Henk for whoever it is that's after him. When I got here nothing happened for days, then you turned up and everything went crazy.'

'I tend to have that effect. It's a gift.' The Doctor gave an amiable shrug. 'So, what were you planning to do when you'd found him? Henk was right about one thing, you were never going to kill him. I don't think you've got a murderous bone in your body.'

'No, I wasn't going to sink to his level. All I had to do was get a positive ID, and transmit the data and coordinates to a pre-set location. As far as I cared, they could deal with him. So long as someone did. That's why I left you when I did. I'd got what I needed. I'm sorry.'

'Oh, you don't want to worry about me. I can take care of myself.'

Emily raised a sarcastic eyebrow at their current predicament. 'Evidently.'

'Most of the time.' He half-smiled. 'What made you come back? You said something about a warning.'

'My employers suggested it would be in my interest to make sure I was off-world before they arrived. To me that didn't sound like they were planning a low-key visit. I couldn't leave without warning you to get out of here too.'

The Doctor frowned. He was grateful to Emily for risking her life to bring him this information, but things were bad enough with Henk and his batch of angry Krillitanes to deal with, let alone some third party with a grudge.

'Doesn't the Agency know who these people are, and why they want Henk so badly?' he asked.

'The deal was made through a broker. It's not unusual

to work on behalf of a client you'll never have any contact with. It's better that way. Keeps things clean. Uncompromised. Dad was pretty diligent, though. He didn't like to go into any situation blind, so when I reached his ship the first thing I did was check his research. He'd compiled a file on Henk. The guy's a pretty shady character, dealing mainly in biological and chemical weapons – the illegal kind. I figured he must have made enemies along the way, but the man has connections, powerful connections across the twelve quadrants. He's virtually untouchable. Whoever's after him must know that.'

'Unless…' The Doctor looked over at Toch'Lu. Unless it wasn't Henk they were really after.

As if nothing untoward had happened, Henk once again took to the stage. There was still a babble of conversation from the delegates, but this quietened as soon as he spoke.

'Friends, thank you for your patience. I must apologise for the lapse in our security procedures, and any discomfort and inconvenience it has caused you. I'm afraid the Calabrian delegation had been infiltrated by anti-government protestors, but the matter has been dealt with and they shan't be bothering us, or anyone else, again.' Henk watched for any adverse reactions, but the delegates were too hungry for the product he was offering to waste any time worrying about an assassination attempt made on someone else. That was the beauty of dealing with interstellar governments, terrorist groups and crime lords – they were far more concerned with their own bigger picture than the value of an individual life, even if it were that of their host.

'Let's get back to business, shall we?' He smiled the broadest of smiles, and spread his arms in a gesture of open friendliness. 'Please welcome Doctor Belima Febron, the scientist behind the greatest advancement in bio-technology in history.'

There was a ripple of applause from those delegates that shared the custom, as Febron stepped forward. She was uncomfortable at the prospect of speaking to such a large audience, and still rattled by Toeclaw's unexpected attack, but her science was sound and her presentation well rehearsed, even if much of the background detail Henk had insisted on including wasn't strictly true. Febron took a deep breath and began.

'This is the most valuable chemical in the universe.' She held up a small vial of Krillitane Oil extract, a carefully directed spotlight causing the yellow liquid inside to sparkle. 'It occurs naturally in only one species, a hunter-gatherer of low intelligence from an undeveloped planet owned by our organisation, a race we have domesticated into manageable livestock. It enables us to harness evolution, to control life's natural imperative to adapt and survive. In effect, we can modify any aspect of our Krillitanes into any configuration we choose. We can increase intelligence, strength, longevity, anything, even endowing psychic abilities or adding an extra toe, and we can do this organically, simply by introducing a specific aspect of mapped genome from any species. The chemical, and evolution, does the rest.' Of course there was no undeveloped planet, no farm containing herds of happy, simple Krillitanes, just the thirteen creatures held against their will in the crypt, but the delegates didn't need to know that. At least with these white lies out of the way she could get back to talking about the science. Ground that Febron felt much safer on.

'We have removed all the uncertainty of existing, outmoded bio-technologies. These are not chimera, unstable genetic combinations of distinct species to create a hybrid. These are not re-engineered clones, prone as they are to psychological and physical defects. This process is an entirely natural biological function of the Krillitanes, a process of natural selection, where evolution chooses the best solution based on your design and criteria, ensuring that the resultant creature is uniquely suited to your needs.

'What's more, I have developed a method of extracting the chemical from our Krillitane stock, and am prototyping a stunning new technology to allow other species to benefit. With your investment and valued support, we will soon have the ability to enable your own species to use this discovery to direct the path of its own evolution. Thank you.'

Relieved, Febron bowed and stepped down from the stage. Henk gave her a wink as he took her place, ready to start talking money with eager potential investors.

Glad that ordeal was over, she was anxious to get back to the crypt and make sure that the Doctor hadn't been interfering with her experiments.

She knew instantly that something was wrong, and the readouts on the monitoring station confirmed her worst fears. While Krillitane Oil was comparatively abundant, the chemical that enabled them to self-evolve was but a tiny proportion of its composition, and it took weeks to extract so much as a thimble of it. This morning the level of extracted fluid had passed fifty per cent, but now it was down to virtually nothing. It could only have been the Doctor.

Febron unlocked the security door and rushed into the crypt. Ignoring the sleeping Krillitanes, she hurried to the extraction system and reached for the vial that should have been half full, wrenching it out of its housing. Empty. Months of patient work, ruined by that inconvenient, interfering Doctor. She would demand to kill him herself for this.

A metallic clang echoed suddenly through the darkness.

Febron spun around. She could see nothing in the dim light of the life-sign monitors. 'Who's there? Branlo, is that you? Tell Henk we have a problem.'

No response. That was strange. Febron walked back towards the antechamber, listening attentively for any repeat of the mysterious noise, but the crypt remained silent.

She stopped as she reached the door, relaxing slightly. It must have been her imagination. Who knew what mischief the Doctor had been up to while he'd been on his own down here? She cursed herself for having left him alone in the first place. Perhaps she should check on the Krillitanes, to be on the safe side.

Examining each enclosure as she came to it, Febron satisfied herself that no further damage had been done. The Krillitanes were still sedated, and extraction of Krillitane Oil hadn't been impeded at source. She turned towards Broken Wing's special enclosure and stopped in her tracks. The enclosure was empty, the chains and pipes that had restrained the powerful male hung limply against the wall. Surely the Doctor hadn't been foolish enough to set him free?

Taking a nervous look around her, Febron hurried over to the enclosure's life-signs monitor.

'Interfering idiot,' she muttered through gritted teeth. The readings indicated that the Doctor had awoken Broken Wing for a short period before sedating him again, but the levels of tranquilliser he'd programmed were nowhere near sufficient to keep this Krillitane under.

A bass, throaty rumble broke the silence, and Febron closed her eyes, sensing Broken Wing was close by, waiting for her.

She had to get out of there, right now.

With a grunt, Febron made a run for it, and immediately heard claws scrambling across the stone floor close behind her. She glanced back. Broken Wing had leapt out of the shadows and was almost upon her. The scientist dived into one of the Krillitane enclosures, pushing her way past the leathery bulk of the sleeping animal. The space was cramped, too cramped for Broken Wing to follow and her only chance of escape. Through into the next enclosure and the next, batting trailing cables out of her way, desperate to reach the door.

A claw suddenly swung at her from above, missing her shoulder by a hair's breadth. Somehow Broken Wing had squeezed himself into the cramped space above the enclosures, crawling across them faster than Febron could negotiate her way through the mass of bodies and technology. She threw herself to the floor, and rolled sideways, back out into the walkway. There, ahead of her and only metres away, was the security door. Febron was on her feet, running blindly. The door was tantalisingly close. Just a few more steps. She could make it. Then, with a crack, she felt her knee joint twist awkwardly and dislocate, her leg snatched out from beneath her, and she fell, face smashing hard into the flagstones.

She reached up, straining for the door, but it was moving away from her. No, she was being pulled back, away from the door, back towards the shadows where Broken Wing had been waiting for her, plotting his revenge.

'Oi, time to wake up, twinkle toes. I know you're earwigging.' The Doctor was standing over the Krillitane, hands in pockets. He gave her foot a light tap with the tip of his trainer and waited. 'No one sleeps that soundly unless they're secretly listening in on a private conversation.'

Reluctantly, Toch'Lu rolled over into a seated position, and smiled defiantly up at him.

The Doctor crouched down, levelling a steely gaze upon the bright blue Calabrian eyes behind which the Krillitane was imprisoned. 'I was talking to your friend. I don't know what his name was – the one with the broken wing. He was telling me that you and your Brood were fugitives when you got mixed up with Henk's mob. Fugitives from whom, I wonder? Mm?'

'It is not of your concern,' Toch'Lu replied, tersely.

'It kind of is, really. You see, there's a ship on its way to this planet, a ship sent by someone who is very eager to trace the whereabouts of our Mister Henk, but I have a theory they're looking for someone else entirely. Someone not so well protected. A fugitive, perhaps. Any ideas?'

'When is this vessel due to arrive?' Toch'Lu had become noticeably paler.

'Could be any time. You look worried.'

Toch'Lu stood up and paced across the room, deep in thought. She stopped and turned to face the Doctor, speaking urgently. 'I need your help. Remove this neck brace so I can assume my Krillitane form. I must free my brethren before that ship arrives.'

'And why would I want to do that? I'm not going to

release a hungry bunch of Krillitanes into the middle of a city packed full of tasty humans, just because you want me to. You didn't even say please.'

The Krillitane stared at the Doctor with disdain. 'My Brood will be the least of this world's concerns if we are still here when that ship makes planetfall.'

'What do you mean?'

'If that vessel is searching for me and not Henk, then we are all dead. Our leader, the Esteemed Father, will stop at nothing to ensure my capture, even the slaughter of every living thing on this pitiful world.'

'Why do I always have to be right?' The Doctor put a hand to his head and ruffled his hair in frustration. 'So what exactly did you do to make him so angry?'

Toch'Lu paced across the room, obviously agitated. 'The Esteemed Father refuses to acknowledge our greater destiny. He is blinkered by the old ways, stuck in the past, but the Krillitane race can be so much more than genetic scavengers. My followers and I had no option but to attempt his overthrow, but we were betrayed, and I was forced into exile.'

She looked up at the high window, lost in bitter memories. 'The leader of the Krillitanes cannot be seen to be weak – his power would be irretrievably undermined. He will see to it that my disloyalty is very publicly punished.'

'If I hadn't come here…' Emily whispered in horror. 'This is all my fault. The people of this city don't stand a chance. It'll be a massacre.'

'You weren't to know. If you hadn't found Henk then somebody else would have, and I might not have been around to sort things out.'

'So more of those creatures are coming, Doctor?' asked Darke.

'More? I should say so. A big fat bunch of more with bells on.' Things had gone from bad to worse, yet again. 'Well, whatever happens, we can't stay locked up in here. Toch'Lu, if I help you, I need you to promise me you'll take your Brood and get off this planet immediately. And I mean right now.'

'I never wished to come here in the first place. You have my word, we shall leave.'

The Doctor dug inside his jacket pocket and pulled out the sonic screwdriver, quickly setting about disabling the device around Toch'Lu's neck. 'You'd better, because if you don't, then you'll have me to answer to.'

The tall oak door smashed open, tearing its hinges from its frame and sending the monks on guard duty flying. Toch'Lu pinned one of them to the floor with her clawed foot, and was about to strike a killing blow when the Doctor grabbed her arm. 'Don't even think about it.'

They hurried out into the deserted nave, and were at the entrance to the crypt in moments. Unlocking the door, the Doctor ushered them through into the antechamber before moving straight to the monitoring station. He slapped on his glasses, and set about the controls. 'Right, first I need to stop the flow of sedatives, get your lot back in the land of the living. Then we need to find a way to get them out of here.'

The Doctor disengaged the locks sealing the security door and pulled it open, turning back towards his companions with a smile. 'You know, I was told once that Worcester is riddled with ancient underground tunnels. Be handy if that were true, wouldn't it?'

'Doctor, look out,' Emily screamed, too late.

Spinning around, the Doctor watched helplessly as Broken Wing hurtled towards the open doorway, blood dripping from his stained teeth.

With a bloodcurdling scream, the Krillitane sprang towards him.

THIRTEEN

There was no way he could have been prepared for the force that slammed into him, knocking him sideways and smashing into the monitoring station.

The Doctor blinked, not entirely sure why he wasn't dead, but a quick survey of his arms and legs found they still seemed to be in full working order, and his suit didn't have a mark on it. His hearts were beating ten to the dozen, but that was only to be expected.

Then he recognised the sound of a struggle behind him. Glancing over his shoulder, he saw two Krillitanes wrestling in the sparking remains of the monitoring station.

Toch'Lu had thrown herself forward, intercepting her fellow Krillitane and saving the Doctor at the last possible moment, and now the Brood Mother had Broken Wing in a grip from which he was unable to free himself.

'Brother Myina, relent,' Toch'Lu roared.

Broken Wing stopped struggling instantly, and looked upon his assailant in shock. 'Brood Mother. It can't be? Henk said he'd…'

'You think that worm has such power that he should defeat me?' Toch'Lu raised her head, haughtily, and then pulled her lips back into a frightening smile. 'It is good to see you again, Brother Myina.'

The Krillitanes touched foreheads, fondly. Then Broken Wing remembered the Doctor. 'Why did you deny me the glory of snapping this treacherous humanoid's neck?' he snarled.

Toch'Lu placed a restraining hand on his chest. 'The Esteemed Father has found us, Brother. The Doctor has agreed to help the Brood escape before his forces arrive.'

'But why must we keep running? The Brood are all but adults. They are strong. Now is the time to stand and fight.'

'Not here, it isn't,' interrupted the Doctor. 'I told you before. I want you off this planet.'

Broken Wing growled at him, but looked to his leader for confirmation that they were to do as the Doctor said. Toch'Lu inclined her head.

'So be it,' the Krillitane conceded, but he had one more score to settle before he was prepared to go anywhere.

Henk stepped out of the Chapter House, and stood at the edge of the small square garden which occupied the centre of the cloisters, watching the snow falling heavily between the buildings.

It had been another long night, and soon dawn would break on a new day. He could finally relax and take a back seat, confident that his legal team would handle contractual negotiations with those delegates who had already agreed to sign licensing deals. Money was about to change hands. Life was good.

Taking a deep breath of the cold night air, he decided to find Febron. She'd been gone for quite a while now, and he wanted her to share in the success of their enterprise. He'd been saving a bottle of fizzy Grokk especially.

As Henk was about to step through the door to the nave, he happened to glance to his left, towards the heavily guarded room where his prisoners were languishing. It was no longer heavily guarded.

'By the Fated Suns... *Branlo!*' Henk bellowed, storming along the corridor. Five guards, all unconscious, lay amongst the shattered ruins of an impregnable oak door. The room itself was empty. Who was this damned Doctor? Some kind of escapologist? Why wouldn't he stay locked up? Henk picked up a stray blaster and primed it.

'Oh my,' Branlo groaned, arriving at the scene of devastation with Archa in tow. 'What happened?'

'Why didn't you pick this up on any of the security-cams?' demanded Henk furiously.

'I... I was monitoring the negotiations, sir. After what happened earlier,' Archa stuttered.

'I warned you before.' Henk raised his blaster and shot Archa in the chest.

The technician staggered backwards, a look of mild surprise on his face, and crumpled to the floor.

'Get the men together and meet me in the nave. We're going after the Doctor and his friends. And clear this mess up before any of the delegates see it.'

'Yes, sir,' whispered Branlo, glancing at the dead body of his friend as he hurried away.

Of all the times for this to happen, thought Henk bitterly. In another few hours the delegates would have been gone, their initial business done, and his carefully laid plans would not now be hanging in peril. The Doctor and Toeclaw would pay for this, and Henk knew exactly where to find them.

First things first. Henk hurried back to the Chapter House doors and quietly locked them. If this was going to get messy, he didn't want any delegates getting involved. Satisfied that the door was secure, he strode purposefully into the nave and headed straight for the crypt. Toeclaw would have no intention of leaving without her precious Brood, and there was only one way out. Then a dreadful thought struck him, and Henk came to a halt.

Belima was almost certainly down there too. Her life, and by default this entire enterprise, was in danger. Suddenly he wasn't so sure what to do.

'That's it. They know we've escaped.' Darke was peering through the keyhole, watching for signs of pursuit.

'The large man is out there. He's looking straight at this door.'

'I'll tell the Doctor,' Emily said, and she slipped into the crypt, averting her eyes from the bloody stain she'd noticed trailing across the floor and into the darkness.

The Doctor was rushing from enclosure to enclosure, having to operate the controls manually now that the main system had been destroyed. She looked nervously over at Toch'Lu and Broken Wing, who were tending to the handful of Krillitanes that had already been roused.

'Everything OK?' asked the Doctor breezily, not losing focus on what he was doing.

Emily swallowed, trying not to worry about the roomful of waking carnivores. 'It's Henk. He knows we're in here. I thought you'd better know.'

The Doctor stopped and looked up. 'Ah. So we'll definitely need another exit then. Hang on a mo.'

He sprinted over to the group of Krillitanes, seemingly unconcerned that there was a strong likelihood they might turn on him without a second thought. 'Toch'Lu. We can't get out the way we came in, but I think there might be a back door. When this place was built there was a secret stairway, hidden in the wall leading up from the crypt to a chamber above the choir. Henk would never have known it was there. We need to find the entrance, and quickly.'

Toch'Lu nodded, and took a pair of younger Krillitanes with her to search the perimeter of the crypt, leaving Broken Wing to watch over the others. He watched the

Brood Mother set to work sniffing out this hidden escape route, and his eyes narrowed.

'Captain Darke.' The Doctor shouted, running over to the antechamber. 'Time to make a strategic withdrawal.'

Giving the Captain room to get past him, the Doctor directed the sonic screwdriver towards the twisted pile of components that had once been the monitoring station. With a pop, the screen began to melt, sparked and burst into flames. 'That should make getting in here a bit trickier. Let's get this door shut and barricaded.'

'What if Toch'Lu can't find the stairway?' Emily asked, slightly alarmed at the speed with which the fire was taking.

The Doctor puffed out his cheeks. 'Not sure. Got any marshmallows?'

Henk came to a decision. Febron's research was well documented and filed, and there were stocks of both Krillitane Oil and its extract stored in the boathouse down by the river. Shame though it would be to face the loss of the scientist, she wasn't indispensable. Much of her work had been completed and could easily be continued by someone else, albeit someone less talented.

It was more important to ensure that the Krillitanes, or at least a few of them, remained unharmed.

'Arm your weapons and get that door open,' he growled.

Branlo rushed forward with the key, turned it in the lock and pulled the door open, ducking back just in time to avoid being roasted by the fireball that exploded ferociously outwards, followed by a billowing cloud of thick, black smoke.

'Well don't just stand there, put it out!' screamed Henk.

'Last one,' said the Doctor, watching the final Krillitane regain consciousness. He was taking a terrible risk, setting them free, but if he could get them to a ship and away there was a chance the Esteemed Father's forces might never touch down, pursuing Toch'Lu off into the stars and as far away from Earth as possible.

'Doctor, we have it.' Toch'Lu was standing beside a thin gap in the masonry, hidden from view behind a pillar.

The Doctor joined her, and peered into the shadows. 'That is brilliant. You'd never even know it existed. Wait here. I'll have a quick look.'

He squeezed through the tiny gap, grateful that this particular crisis had happened during his tenth life. Heaven help them all if it had been his sixth. He still couldn't look at a carrot-based diet drink without feeling queasy.

Thankfully, the tight passage opened onto a stairway that would accommodate all of them, and the Doctor scurried up the spiralling staircase until he came to the top. Crouching low, he peered over the parapet. Henk's men had fetched extinguishers. There wasn't much time.

Down below, Emily was getting worried. 'Doctor,

where are you?' she half-whispered, half-shouted, jumping back as the Doctor's head suddenly popped through the gap in front of her.

'Give us a chance.' He gave Emily a wink, and clambered back into the crypt. 'Right, there's room enough for everyone. Be quiet when you get to the top. From the balcony we can reach one of the upper windows and get out of here. Off you go.'

The Doctor sent Emily up first, but held Darke back for a moment, passing him the test tube of Krillitane Oil extract. 'Take this. Remember what I told you, it's lethal to them. Keep it safe and only use it as a last resort,' he whispered urgently. Darke nodded in understanding, before following Emily into the secret passage.

'Righty-ho, then. Unless you fancy toasting your wings, I suggest you get a wriggle on.' The Doctor ushered the eleven drowsy Krillitanes through the gap, followed by Toch'Lu and finally Broken Wing.

'I really must visit this place when it's not crawling with aliens,' said the Doctor with a sniff, taking one last look at the graceful arches of the crypt before sliding back through the gap and bounding up the hidden staircase.

At the top, the Doctor immediately noticed a change in the Krillitanes. They seemed to have split into two camps, with four of them gathering around Broken Wing, clinging to the parapet like gargoyles overlooking the choir. Toch'Lu and Broken Wing were staring at each other, silent and angry. The female shook her head, but Broken Wing had made his decision. Supported by two of the others, he leapt over the edge. Two more Krillitanes took to their wings and flew high towards the vaulted ceiling.

The Doctor rushed forwards, but there was nothing he could do.

Toch'Lu stepped over to the parapet, watching her mate swoop down towards Henk and his men. 'I commanded him not to do this, but there is Krillitane honour to be upheld. He would not be swayed.'

'It's you the Esteemed Father is after, not Broken Wing, so nothing has changed,' the Doctor replied grimly. If need be he would return to deal with this situation once the most pressing danger was dealt with. 'Let's get you to that Calabrian ship.'

The Krillitanes glided silently above their targets, unseen, unheard, until, at a signal from Broken Wing, they began to dive.

It was only a matter of luck that Henk happened to roll his eyes to the heavens in desperation, only to see three winged creatures bearing down upon him. He fired two shots from his blaster, both of them pummelling into the Krillitane on the left. Breaking away from Broken Wing, it spiralled out of control and slammed into a row of pews, the crash alerting Henk's men to the attack.

One Krillitane alone was unable to support the weight of Broken Wing, and they immediately lost altitude, sweeping dangerously close to the floor. At the last possible second, she let go of her burden and swung back towards the ceiling to regroup, her task accomplished. Broken Wing hit the ground lightly on all fours, alert and sniffing for Henk's distinctive scent.

Henk had already recognised his imminent danger and fled towards the cloisters as soon as he'd fired his weapon. There was no longer any point kidding himself. This whole deal had gone belly-up, and he wasn't going to stick around while those vile monsters picked at its carcass.

'It's higher than you'd think, isn't it?' observed the Doctor, looking through the window they'd just broken and across the snow-covered Cathedral roof. 'And we're not even at the top.'

Emily was good with heights, but she knew her limits. 'There is no way we're going to get down there without breaking our necks. If we slip, that's it.'

'Then we shall carry you,' Toch'Lu offered.

'What did she just say?' Emily glared at the Doctor, pretty certain she'd understood exactly what Toch'Lu was planning.

'Whatever you do, don't let go,' advised the Doctor, allowing Toch'Lu to wrap her arms around him. Emily and Darke exchanged worried glances, as bony Krillitane fingers took hold of them and lifted them from their feet. Suddenly they were flying, swooping away from the Cathedral and into the snowstorm.

The ride was exhilarating. Snowflakes and the bitter, icy wind bit against the Doctor's skin, but he welcomed the winter storm that would surely enable them to pass beyond the city walls unnoticed. The Doctor looked back and was satisfied that Emily and Darke were close behind, though the Captain did not look at all happy.

Then the sky fell in.

A blinding white light flooded across the dawn sky, accompanied by a blast of superheated air and a pressure wave that sent the fugitives tumbling towards the river. As Toch'Lu struggled to regain control, the Doctor caught a glimpse of a deep-space frigate dropping belly first through the storm clouds, directly over the Cathedral. The ship's retro-thrusters beat down on full power, slowing its descent to a halt mere metres above the Cathedral tower. Snow melted away from the vast roof in an instant from the intense heat.

The ship hovered for a moment, its size making it look like an airborne reflection of the Cathedral itself, then a flicker of light flashed on the underside of the hull. A hatch opened, from which tiny figures spilled out and onto the tower, crawling fluidly over the ancient stone.

Krillitanes. Dozens of them.

The Doctor looked on in horror. His gamble hadn't paid off, and now they were in serious trouble.

Inside the Cathedral, all hell had broken loose.

The pitched battle between Broken Wing's supporters and Henk's people was suddenly thrown into disarray as the windows that ran along the length of the Cathedral shattered spectacularly inwards, too weak to withstand the shockwave pushed out by the Krillitane frigate's retro-thrusters. The deafening howl of straining engines bounced off the Cathedral walls, an echoing cacophony that sent those Krillitanes that were airborne crashing to the floor, writhing in pain and unable to avoid the shards of glass that rained upon them like a million daggers.

In the cloisters, Broken Wing stumbled into a wall, clutching at his head to protect it from the noise. Henk couldn't believe his luck as he watched the Krillitane collapse to the floor. The damn thing had almost had him cornered. Whatever was happening, it had at least saved him from this particular fate.

Blinking in the harsh light, Henk scrambled across to the edge of the cloisters and peered upwards. 'What in the name of… Who the hell's that?'

Henk watched as the ship veered away towards the south, no doubt about to touch down in the open area between the Cathedral and the Castle. That cut him off from his planned escape route, via the boathouse and the river. He'd have to make his way out through the city instead.

Grateful that the hideous noise had abated, he wondered why the pilot had seen fit to make such a spectacular arrival, but then a groan from the floor alerted him that Broken Wing was beginning to recover his senses. It must have been the pitch of the engines that had floored him, realised Henk.

No time to waste on making grand plans. He needed a diversion and a bolthole. Then he heard angry shouts, and fists banging against a door, and he remembered the delegates were still locked away in the Chapter House. Henk sprinted over and wrenched the brace from its housing. The doors swung open and he dived into the rush of delegates as they spilled out into the cloisters, pushing them out of the way, desperate to put as many of them between himself and Broken Wing as possible.

The room was a mess. A few windows on the Cathedral side were now little more than gaping holes, and the floor was littered with glass. The Octulans were still in their pressurised bubble, quivering with fear. Their travelpods had been knocked aside during the panic. Henk couldn't care less. It was every man, or blob, for himself. And if the bubble still had power, then so did the other tech in the room, which meant Henk still had an ace up his sleeve.

Broken Wing staggered to his feet and shook his head to clear it. He looked up at the Cathedral tower, keen eyes picking out the grey and brown skins of Krillitane, pouring into the gaping windows at the top. The Esteemed Father's death squad.

He could only hope that, by now, Toch'Lu would be moving away from the city, to safety. He would confront the death squad, hold them here for as long as possible, then there was still a chance she might make it. But first he wanted Henk, and the terrified screaming coming from the opposite side of the cloisters told the Krillitane where to find him.

He bounded across the garden, jaws snapping at any

of the aliens that happened to stumble into his path, through the doors into the Chapter House. Broken Wing slid to a standstill and hissed. There was Henk, climbing onto a raised platform, laughing for reasons best known to himself. The Krillitane hissed again and crept forward, glass crackling under his long feet.

'Come on, then.' Henk waved, a victorious smile on his face, secure in the knowledge that the stage's force wall was activated and in full working order. He was quite safe from this stupid animal. 'Tasty Mister Henk. Come on.'

Broken Wing tensed his muscles, ready to pounce. Then a voice stopped him dead.

'Brother Myina, disgraced First Minister and consort to the treacherous Toch'Lu, how wonderful to see you again. It's been too long.'

Standing on the threshold of the Chapter House was a Krillitane, wingless, taller and broader than Broken Wing by some measure, and with the bearing of a leader.

Broken Wing hissed, lips drawing back, baring his fangs. 'You.'

FOURTEEN

'That was too close. Do you think they spotted us?' Emily wondered.

The Doctor was watching the ship through the telescopic site he'd taken from Emily's rifle. 'I shouldn't have thought so. Until they broke through the cloud cover they wouldn't have been able to see a thing, and they'd have been far too focused on pulling off their big arrival to worry about us. I'd guess they targeted the coordinates you sent them and went for it. Shock and Awe.'

'You're not kidding,' she replied.

The dishevelled group had gone to ground in an area of scrubby woodland just south of the Castle, where they watched as the Krillitane frigate settled on its landing gear.

Darke was horrified to see more dreadful creatures pouring out of the giant metal monster, swarming into the Cathedral. 'When they don't find what they're looking for, they'll be certain to search the city. The people are defenceless. It will be a bloodbath.' His face hardened. He was not going to allow this to happen. 'I have to get back to the Castle, mobilise my troops and evacuate the city. The southern gate is not far from here.'

'Sounds like a plan, Captain. I'm coming with you. Emily, go back to your ship, get out of here. This isn't your fight.'

'Not my fight?' she protested. 'Doctor, all of this is my fault. It's my responsibility. And I'm not leaving you again.'

The Doctor sighed. 'All right. Blimey. Just keep close, OK? And don't go all heroic on me.' He gave her a smile, knowing there was no point in making an argument of it.

Toch'Lu was a short distance away, deep in conversation with her Brood. She brushed foreheads with each of them in turn, and the Doctor realised they were sharing a final moment together, saying their last goodbyes.

One by one, the Krillitanes took to the air, leaving Toch'Lu standing alone, head bowed. Then, with a shake of her wings, she reformed into the shape of a generic human female, a peasant girl, and walked back to join the others.

'I have sent them to the Calabrian ship, with

instructions to leave this planet and never return,' she said simply.

'You're not going with them?' asked the Doctor quietly.

'I cannot. If I remain with them, then the lives of my children will never be safe.' Toch'Lu looked towards the imposing Cathedral, calm and determined. 'My consort remains within that place. I would join him. Brother Myina was right, we cannot run from our destiny for ever.'

The Doctor surveyed his troops. 'Right, then. Four of us, far too many of them. Pretty much business as usual. Lead the way, mon Capitan.'

After all the strange adventures of the last few days, Captain Darke was almost glad to be returning to an endeavour he knew so well, but had thought he'd left behind him long ago – preparing for war.

As they passed through the southern gate, he ordered the guards to forget about manning their posts and follow him. There was little point protecting the Castle against marauders when a greater threat was already well within the city walls. He needed every man who could bear arms.

When they reached the main building, the Captain's presence immediately lifted the spirits of the garrison, who had been milling about in a state of confusion, unsure what to do about the lights in the sky that had surely been the wrath of God.

Butcher was one of the first to approach him, on the verge of panic. 'Captain, we've been up the tower, sir. The Cathedral is overrun with monstrosities, perversions of God's creatures. Is this the End of Days, sir?'

Darke barely understood what was happening himself, but he decided to keep things simple for his men, who had not had the benefit of the Doctor's company. 'This is not God's work, nor the Devil's. These are creatures from far shores, Dog-heads from the East in the employ of the Empress Matilda, who is intent on taking this city from King Stephen.'

'Two opposing forces fighting for the throne,' the Doctor murmured quietly to Toch'Lu. 'Sound familiar?'

'We must evacuate the city,' the Captain ordered. 'Take half of the men and form them into groups of six, then fan outwards from the Cathedral. Clear every building. I want every man, woman and child beyond those city walls. Tell them to find cover, keep warm and stay hidden. Then regroup and head back to the city. Be prepared for a fight.'

'Yes, sir. You can count on me, sir.' Butcher hurried away, calmed by Darke's authority and determined to carry out his orders to the letter.

Darke turned back to the Doctor 'We have forty men at our disposal. I take it we march on the Cathedral?' he asked.

The Doctor nodded. 'They'll have had time to do a thorough search by now. It won't be long before they make a start on the city. The best you can do is set up a defensive perimeter along Lich Street and Bishops Street, stop the Krillitanes from breaking through for long enough to complete the evacuation.'

'You will need to arm yourselves, of course,' Darke observed. While Emily's padded armour looked sound, the strange, simple garb of the Doctor would offer no protection in the heat of battle.

'I'm afraid this is where we part company, Captain. We'll be fighting on a different front.'

For a moment Darke didn't understand, and then he realised the Doctor planned to accompany Toch'Lu and return to the Cathedral. The selfless bravery of this man was astounding. 'Then good fortune to you, Doctor. My lady.'

The Captain bowed and took his leave. They watched him go, rallying the troops as he went.

'And then there were three,' said Emily, softly.

'Bow before your leader,' the newcomer demanded, a chilly disdain in his voice.

'Never,' Broken Wing spat back. In a blur of rage, he hurled himself at his sworn enemy, but the Esteemed Father was stronger, faster, stepping neatly to one side and striking a crashing blow to Broken Wing's skull. Dazed, the Krillitane staggered and fell.

The Esteemed Father was on him in an instant, digging his claws into the scruff of Broken Wing's neck, making sure he drew blood. 'Do not dare to disobey me again,' he whispered, and released his grip.

From the safety of the stage, Henk watched unhappily as a dozen more Krillitanes, again wingless and as muscular as the first, hurried into the room, fanning out and encircling the dazed Broken Wing, ensuring he had no means of escape. They ignored Henk completely, and he realised with some relief that they seemed to have no interest in him whatsoever.

Another Krillitane entered, slighter in build than any of the others, with thin flexible fingers and a more bulbous snout. Henk decided it must be some kind of specialised tracker. Febron's science had been right on the money.

The tracker approached its leader deferentially. 'Esteemed Father, we have completed our search of the building. We found four bodies, members of the traitor's Brood, along with a group of humanoids. There was evidence of a conflict between them, but we can find no sign of the traitor.'

The Esteemed Father's nostrils flared as he digested this information. 'Then widen the search beyond the walls of this temple. Rip every fetid dwelling in this outpost apart, if you have to. Just find her.' He watched the tracker slip away, and returned his attention to their captive, observing the fugitive's scarred and battered body, the bent and broken wing that hung limply behind the Krillitane's back. A member of the new generation of airborne upstarts who considered themselves the natural successors to his throne, whether he was ready to relinquish it or not. 'The years have not been kind, have they, Brother Myina? Or are your injuries the result of some domestic dispute?'

Broken Wing curled his lip, wondering if he might have another opportunity to tear out his enemy's throat with his teeth before his personal guard could react. 'If you are going to kill me, then do it now before I have to endure any more of your insufferable pomposity.'

'Myina the Orator.' The Esteemed Father laughed. 'How we miss your presence on the Council. It has always been a matter of great sorrow to us that you chose to side with our cousin. You were a powerful and respected First Minister. You could regain that position, if you were to tell us where the traitor is hiding.'

'You're wasting your time, *Esteemed Father*,' Broken Wing laughed, his words loaded with sarcasm. 'She was never even here. Our group was separated, months ago. The four younglings and I were ensnared by traders and sold on. The Brood Mother escaped. I don't know where to, but she's beyond your pitiful reach.'

'I think not,' sniffed the Esteemed Father. 'Her filthy scent is all over you. We shall find her, whether or not you provide us with assistance.'

'Ahem,' Henk coughed. 'Perhaps I can be of service?'

Safe as he felt for now, protected by his force wall, Henk knew he couldn't stay behind it for ever. If it were possible to broker a deal with this obviously important Krillitane, he might even get out of this in one piece.

The Esteemed Father turned, as if noticing Henk for the first time.

'Allow me to introduce myself. I am Lozla Nataniel Henk, and—'

'I know who you are,' the Krillitane leader hissed.

Henk bowed in mock humbleness. 'My reputation precedes me.'

'Your reputation is built on exploitation and murder, and your crimes against the Krillitanes will not go unpunished. I have had agents scouring the galaxy, searching for Sister Toch'Lu and her cabal of conspirators. Once my agents discovered you had enslaved them, all we had to do was find you.' The Esteemed Father pointed a finely manicured claw at Henk. 'Execute him.'

A Krillitane immediately broke ranks and sprang towards the stage. With a bolt of energy, the force wall repelled the creature, hurling it backwards across the floor. It lay still where it fell, smoke drifting slowly from the corpse.

'Oh, dear. Do you think he'll recover?' Henk's face was a mask of compassion. 'I am terribly sorry about that. The stage is protected by a force wall, you see. I can't believe I forgot to mention it.' He had taken the precaution of increasing the defence level to full power as soon as he'd reached the controls.

Hissing, the Esteemed Father stalked to the foot of the stage, eyes blazing with hatred for this puny being.

Henk continued with rather more confidence than he felt. Fortunately, empty bravado was his stock in trade. 'Now, as I understand it, you're looking for the female. Toeclaw?'

'Toch'Lu,' the Krillitane spat back, angered by the mispronunciation.

'Indeed. So knowledge of her whereabouts is therefore something that would be of great value to you?'

'I will take great pleasure in ending your worthless life, Henk.' Broken Wing interrupted, bitterly, but Henk ignored him. Broken Wing was obviously not the main player here.

'My thought is this. If I had such information, then perhaps we could come to some kind of arrangement?' Henk licked his lips, nervously. 'Let me return to my ship, unharmed, and I'll tell you exactly where to find your traitor. How does that sound?'

Opening his mouth wide, the Esteemed Father revealed a double row of razor-sharp teeth, and let out a hideous, guttural cackle. His jaws snapped shut with a crunch and he glared hungrily at Henk.

As Darke led his men towards Friar Street, he found it difficult to believe that in happier times it had been filled with the bustle of everyday life. This cold morning, however, saw a steady stream of scared people surging towards the city gate at Sidbury. The old, the young, traders struggling with carts overloaded with goods, a desperate mother reassuring her distraught child, all desperate to escape the city.

His small army found the going hard. The crush of people impeded the troops' progress, and the heavy snowfall didn't make things any easier. Bishops Street was on the opposite side of the Cathedral to the Castle, and although the distance wasn't far, the Captain feared they would not make it in time if they continued along their current path.

Leaving a group of soldiers to defend this part of the road, Darke took the rest of his troops through a deserted building and across the arable plots running between the row of houses and the Cathedral grounds. As they moved quietly past, the Captain surveyed its walls, now devoid of the ungodly figures that had so recently swept across them. How strange that those pale walls, a symbol of all that was good and righteous in the world, could now contain such devilry.

Within minutes they had reached Lich Street, where the Cathedral's main gatehouse would afford them some advantage over the Krillitanes. Darke split his remaining men into three groups, sending one towards the end of Bishops Street and another further along the High Street. These would be the second line of defence as and when their foe overcame Darke's own unit, who would do their utmost to defend the gatehouse for as long as possible by engaging the enemy within the walls of the Cathedral.

They didn't have long to wait.

Wolf-like shadows scurried through the arched Cathedral entrance, ugly black stains racing across the deep white snow. In no time the first wave was almost upon them.

'This is it, lads. Fight to your last breath,' Darke murmured, crossing himself in spite of his dented faith.

Still, if it turned out there was a higher being watching over them after all, it wouldn't hurt to show willing. They were going to need all the help they could get.

He raised his sword above his head and bellowed to his men, 'For the King!'

Charging out of their hiding place beyond the gatehouse, Darke's vastly outnumbered force ploughed indomitably into the oncoming enemy. The battle for the city had begun.

The Doctor, Emily and Toch'Lu were creeping up a slipway, leading from the banks of the River Severn into the south-west corner of the Cathedral grounds. They were relieved to find that the Krillitanes had not thought to place any guards in this otherwise deserted area.

The river served a dual purpose for the Castle: as a natural defence against attack from the west, and as a means of delivering vital supplies during times of siege. It now offered the perfect clandestine route back into the Cathedral for the Doctor and his group, who had left the Castle via the riverbank, moving quickly along it until they reached the riverside entrance to the Cathedral. They hid in the shadow of the boathouse, a hundred metres from where the Krillitane vessel had touched down.

'So, we're in. What now?' asked Emily, scanning the Cathedral for an entrance. A door in the side of the refectory, not far from their hiding place, looked promising. She shivered. 'Somewhere out of this weather would be a good start.'

At the same moment they both realised they were standing right beside the door into the boathouse. 'How about in here?' said the Doctor, and they ducked inside, grateful for the building's relative warmth.

'That is so much better.' Emily hugged herself.

'Blimey.' The Doctor had immediately taken an interest in the vessel stored inside the boathouse. It was no boat. 'Property of one Mister Henk.'

An eight-metre-long industrial hover skiff rested on its landing skids, taking up almost the entire space. What's more, it was fully laden with barrels.

'Just what the doctor ordered.' Smiling, the Doctor bounded aboard and checked its flight controls. A plan was already formulating at the back of his mind. 'Henk's entire stock of Krillitane Oil.'

Toch'Lu hung back by the doorway, nervously, and Emily couldn't help but notice. 'Are you OK?' she asked. The Krillitane glanced at the rows of barrels.

The Doctor tapped one of the barrels. 'What we have here is the one thing that the Krillitane fear. Their own oil. It's what made them who they are, except it's become lethal to them. If one drop touches their skin, just one drop, it causes an immediate and catastrophic anaphylactic reaction.'

'It kills them?'

'Well,' the Doctor swallowed. 'It kind of makes them explode. Not a nice way to go.' While this discovery was useful, he had no intention of using it other than as a last resort.

The Doctor leapt down from the skiff and approached Toch'Lu. 'I'd say what we do now is up to you. If you can get your fellow Krillitanes to leave this world unharmed, just leave, then I'm not going to have to use that stuff. But if you can't…'

Toch'Lu shook off her human disguise, her orange eyes blazing in their deep sockets. She understood what he was asking of her. 'That any of my Brood lives is thanks to your actions. Whatever happens, I will stand by my promise to you, Doctor. Much depends upon whom the Esteemed Father has sent after me, and whether they have orders to take me alive. If I cannot negotiate, then I will fight.'

'I can't give you long,' warned the Doctor.

'Then let us begin. I will see to it that by morning none of my brethren remain on this world. If that means all must die, then so be it,' she replied.

They left the boathouse and hurried over to the open doorway Emily had located earlier. In the distance, the screams and shouts of a pitched battle sounded eerily flat, deadened by the thick snow that lay like a death shroud over the city. Emily thought of Captain Darke, not daring to hope he would be fortunate enough to survive.

Once inside, they found the refectory was deserted. Banks of equipment installed by Henk's people had been smashed and rendered inoperable by the Krillitanes, who had stormed through like a plague of locusts. Here and there dead bodies were scattered, no longer in need of Henk's promised payday.

Toch'Lu sped ahead, stopping at the next set of doors, snout lifted, testing the air. She tensed suddenly, then bolted out into the cloisters without warning, leaving the Doctor and Emily staring at each other in shock. As one, they sprinted after her, just in time to see her tail disappear around the corner.

'What's got into her?' the Doctor shouted as he pounded along the corridor. 'Looks like she's heading for the Chapter House.'

'You mean you don't know what Henk has been keeping in there?' Emily replied, as they reached the doorway and staggered to a halt. She blinked, surprised at what she saw. 'Oh. Actually, that wasn't what I was expecting.'

Bizarrely, Henk stood on stage as if ready to continue his sales pitch, even though the delegates were now either dead or fleeing the planet in their ships. He almost looked relieved to see the Doctor and Emily, and she could see why.

Half a dozen nervous-looking Krillitanes stood around the edge of the Chapter House, not sure what to do about the situation unfolding before them, and there, at the centre of the room, Toch'Lu stretched her wings in a display of superiority, circling an imperious-looking Krillitane who looked upon her with disdain.

'Well, well, well,' sneered the Esteemed Father, not taking his eyes off his mortal foe. 'It seems there is no longer any need for us to make a deal, Mister Henk.'

FIFTEEN

The bitter enemies stared at each other intently, waiting to see who would betray a sign of weakness, who would be the first to blink. The tension spread to all those watching, even Henk, who still couldn't comprehend how the last twenty-four hours had panned out quite so badly.

'Cousin.' The Esteemed Father nodded, welcoming his avowed enemy graciously, attention focused entirely on Toch'Lu.

'Esteemed Father,' Toch'Lu hissed back, her voice dripping with hatred. 'I am honoured that you consider me such a threat that you choose to face me in person.'

'There are only so many stones in the universe. One is bound to uncover a base coward skulking beneath one of them without undue effort.' The Esteemed Father shook his head, his snout wrinkled as if her very existence created a foul odour. 'It gives me no pleasure to find you here. That you allowed yourself and your Brood to be imprisoned by this… parasite. You are not fit to be called Krillitane.'

'And you are not fit to rule us.'

Outside, the Doctor put a finger to his lips, making it clear that he wanted Emily to stay safely out of view, then he adjusted his tie and strode brazenly into the Chapter House.

'All right, calm down, calm down. If all you're going to do is trade bon mots all morning, we'll be here till lunchtime.'

This unannounced intrusion incensed the Krillitane leader. 'Who dares address the Esteemed Father without due deference?'

'That'll be me. I'm the Doctor, and I don't do due deference. Actually, I can barely say it. You must be, what, the Emperor of the Krillitanes or something?' The Doctor looked the Esteemed Father up and down. He was naked, as was the Krillitane way. 'I don't want to speak out of turn, but your robes aren't up to much, are they? Are they new? I think you should have a word with your tailor.'

'Your scent is familiar to me.' The Esteemed Father frowned. He was certain he had never encountered this insolent creature. No, this was more of a race memory, a scent passed from one generation to the next, warning of danger. And then he remembered.

'A Time Lord? How intriguing. It is rare indeed to encounter one of your kind, since they passed into myth.'

'Big old universe, busy diary. You should think yourself lucky I found a window in my schedule.'

The momentary distraction caused by the Doctor's entrance was all Toch'Lu needed, and she exchanged a surreptitious signal with Broken Wing before the Esteemed Father's eyes turned back towards her.

'I have no enmity with you, Time Lord. I advise you to return to whichever dusty library you hail from, before I have reason to do so.' The Esteemed Father turned away from the newcomer, dismissing him from his mind.

All levity had gone from the Doctor's voice when he spoke again. 'The internal politics of the Krillitanes have no place on Earth. I warn you now, gather your troops and take your argument back to your homeworld.'

'Or what? You think I should fear you, Time Lord?'

'Try me.'

Suddenly, Broken Wing launched himself at the guard nearest to him, snapping its long neck and hurling its lifeless body into the others before they had a chance to react. At the same moment, Toch'Lu flew at the Esteemed Father, digging her claws deep into his flesh and lifting him off his feet, up towards the high ceiling and through one of the smashed windows.

'So much for a diplomatic solution,' the Doctor murmured. He was about to leave when he remembered Henk was still on the stage. But when he looked over,

Henk had already gone, having made good use of the chaos to escape unnoticed.

The Doctor stepped backwards, just in time, as Broken Wing slammed into the ground where he'd been standing, locked in a vicious struggle with another of the guards.

Then a deafening round of blaster fire shot through the air. The Doctor ducked on impulse, searching desperately for the source of the gunfire. He caught sight of Henk firing another parting shot as he ran out of the door, but the shot went wide of the mark. Too wide, and the Doctor realised that neither he nor the Krillitanes had been Henk's intended target at all. So who or what had been?

A resounding clunk, followed by a skittering, cracking sound emanated from the opposite end of the room, something rupturing. The Doctor looked towards the reflective slab which he'd taken to be some kind of oversized display screen.

Creeping across its surface, cracks joined and spread rapidly, black liquid crystal seeping through them, dripping downwards. The whole thing had taken on the appearance of melting candle wax.

Then something smashed through, what looked like a tail, creating an explosion of black shards.

'Right,' was all the Doctor could manage, gawping in disbelief at what he was seeing, before gathering his wits and running for his remaining lives.

Henk's creature, the Krillitane Storm, stalked out

of the wreckage of its enclosure, towering above his genetic cousins. It let out a bloodcurdling scream, lifting its head high on its long, muscular neck, surveying its new surroundings. Then it struck, plucking one of the cowering Krillitane guards from the floor and crushing the unfortunate individual in its powerful jaws.

Safely outside, the Doctor slammed the doors shut and locked them. They wouldn't stop that thing for long. Ruffling his fingers through his hair, he looked around for Emily, but there was no sign of her. 'Why do they never stay where I tell them?' the Doctor sighed. She must have seen Henk leave and gone after him on her own, and if Henk was looking for a quick escape, he'd be heading for the boathouse. Hoping Emily wasn't going to try anything stupid, he sprinted off along the cloisters.

Broken Wing and the guard he'd been fighting fell away from each other and stared up at the abomination before them, not sure whether to feel kinship or revulsion.

At the same moment they both realised that, if they wanted to live, then this fight was over. The guard crawled to his feet and fled, scrambling up the Chapter House wall and out through a broken window. Broken Wing was not far behind, and he pulled himself onto the building's conical roof, searching the sky for any sign of where Toch'Lu had dragged their foe.

A shriek, followed by the clatter of falling masonry, caused him to look towards the tower. There, at the top, he could see them, dangerously close to the edge, as the

Esteemed Father landed a crippling blow which almost sent Toch'Lu tumbling over the side.

Broken Wing leapt from the roof to the exterior wall of the Cathedral, and began to climb upwards, lamenting his inability to fly. The Brood Mother was strong, without doubt, but she had been weakened by her captivity. He had to get up there, as fast as possible, otherwise she would not survive.

Henk half-dragged, half-pushed Emily through the refectory doors and out into the grounds, the blunt muzzle of his blaster pressed hard against her ribs. He'd grabbed the girl outside the Chapter House, recognising the need for a back-up plan, some protection in case releasing his pet monster hadn't finished the Doctor and the Krillitanes off as hoped. The amount of development money he'd poured into that beast, he was determined to get some value out of it.

'What is it with men and guns?' Emily struggled against his grip, determined to make this as difficult for him as possible. 'You're pathetic. Half the man my dad was.'

'Well he's dead, isn't he?'

'So are you,' she spat back.

'Emily!'

They stopped short, hearing the Doctor's voice shout out from somewhere inside the building. Emily was about to call back in response, but felt Henk's blaster digging into her.

'Don't even think about it,' he growled, pulling her through the snow towards the boathouse.

'You don't seriously think you're going to get out of here in one piece, do you?' Emily smirked, no longer afraid of the man. He was nothing more than a coward and a bully. 'If the Doctor doesn't get you, the Krillitanes will.'

'Just shut your mouth and walk.' Henk kicked open the boathouse door and all but threw Emily onto the skiff, her head clanging against one of the barrels. She remained where she fell, out cold, and Henk stepped indifferently past her, jumping into the pilot's seat to power up its antigrav engines.

Henk gunned the engines to full power. The vehicle juddered into life, lifted off its skids and shunted backwards at speed, knocking the boathouse doors violently out of the way.

Wrestling with the controls, Henk swung the skiff in a wide arc, bringing its nose around so it was pointing towards the slipway. So intent on escape was he that he didn't see the Doctor burst through the refectory door nearby.

'Oh no you don't,' bellowed the Doctor, storming after the vehicle, ignoring the stinging pinpricks of snow being kicked up by the antigrav's backdraft. Gritting his teeth, he took a flying leap as the skiff hit the slipway and dipped down towards the river, just managing to grab hold of its loading arm as it rode out over the surface of the Severn, in a wash of spray.

Immediately the Doctor felt his grip slipping. His feet were dragging through the skiff's choppy wake, its foaming, icy fingers pulling at him, threatening to yank him into the murky depths. Grimacing with strain, he wrenched his legs away from the water, barely wrapping them around the loading arm in time as his fingers slipped, and he found himself dangling upside down, waves whipping at his hair.

'On the plus side,' he thought, 'at least that leaves my hands free.' In a flash, the Doctor had the sonic screwdriver pointed at a control box, and the loading arm began to swing around with a whine of servos, sweeping towards Henk, who remained oblivious to the presence of his additional passenger.

'Hello, stranger!' cried the Doctor, arms open wide as if ready to embrace an old friend.

Henk's eyes widened in shock, noticing too late as the loading arm swept towards him, carrying its insanely grinning payload. The two bodies slammed into one another, and the next thing Henk knew he was on the deck, tangled beneath a mass of bony limbs and an enormously long overcoat. He kicked hard, his boot connecting with the Doctor's chest, sending the interfering fool flying. Henk scrambled to his feet, blaster in hand, and waved it menacingly in the Doctor's direction.

'I've just about had enough of you,' Henk shouted wildly, his face crimson, the personification of rage. Flecks of saliva flew from his mouth, as he poured all his anger and frustration towards the Doctor. 'Do you have any idea how much money I could have made out of this little number? Do you? Between you and that rancid Krillitane witch, you've ruined everything. Everything.'

Sprawled on the deck, the Doctor looked angrily back at Henk. 'What you were doing was wrong. Beyond unethical. What's worse, Febron knew it and still carried on. The Krillitanes are sentient beings. Whatever they've done, however ruthless they are, they still have rights.'

'I couldn't give a Pescaton's scaly fin for Krillitane rights. No amount of ethics will buy you your own solar system, Doctor. For all I care, they can kill each other and any stinking Earthling that gets in their way. But you know what? You, I'm going to take great pleasure in killing myself.'

With a cold, unpleasant sneer, Henk raised his blaster and took aim.

Unaware of events transpiring within the Cathedral, the Krillitane horde had overcome Captain Darke's defensive forces, thundering onwards over the bodies of the dead.

'Captain, they've breached the wall,' shouted one of the men, as Darke wearily pulled his sword from the belly of a felled beast, one of so many they had slain. The Krillitanes surely hadn't expected to encounter such a spirited opposition, he reflected, proud of his men.

A hiss, terrifyingly close, alerted the Captain to another attack, and he swung round to find a Krillitane bearing down upon him, fangs glistening. He stumbled backwards, struggling to lift his sword, but there was no time. Then, with a thump and a whimper, the creature tumbled to one side, a pike embedded in its back. Darke breathed a sigh of relief, as young Miller retrieved the weapon that had just saved his life. They took refuge behind its lifeless body.

Exhausted, Miller panted, 'What shall we do? There are too many off them.'

'Keep your head up, lad. We're not finished yet,' Darke reassured him. But the young man was right: they were vastly outnumbered, and clearly this line of defence had failed. Yet even with the casualties they had suffered, they had brought down a great many Krillitanes, and the Captain drew strength from that fact. 'However bad this gets, these beasts are not invincible.'

Already the last of the Krillitanes were at the wall, scaling it with ease and moving onto the buildings beyond. The battle would have to move on, into the city.

'Miller, find any of the men who can still fight. We need to regroup, chase the devils down and attack them from behind, while our secondary line engages them at the High Street.'

'Sir.' Miller got to his feet and made off towards the gate, where a few of the troops were already gathering.

Darke dragged himself up and began to follow Miller, but he'd barely gone five paces when a new sound echoed from within the Cathedral, a howl, deeper and more threatening than the bat-like hiss of the Krillitanes. Miller and the other men heard it too, and looked to their commander, unsure what to do.

The Captain tightened his grip on the hilt of his sword, listening, waiting for any sign of the source of that tremendous noise. For a moment there was nothing, save for the deafening silence that followed all battles, and then the howl rang out again, closer this time. Much closer.

Toch'Lu pitched and took another dive at the Esteemed Father, but her strike was parried by the larger Krillitane, and he slashed at her right wing, claws ripping through the thin web of skin as she flew past. The wing was ruined, little more than shredded rags, and it was all Toch'Lu could do to remain in the air long enough to find her footing on the sloping roof without smashing into it.

'If your forebears could only witness the lack of respect you show the Beast of Bessan, they would be ashamed,' the Esteemed Father snarled, stalking Toch'Lu as she fought to regain her balance. 'Your generation, so thrilled with the power of flight, you think those wings are a mark of your superiority.'

'They are a symbol of progress, of the future, to those of us who recognise the true destiny of the Krillitanes,' Toch'Lu snapped back, edging towards the apex of the tower, desperate to retain some tactical advantage over her rival by holding the upper ground.

The Esteemed Father feigned a lunge at his opponent, gaining a little ground on her in the process. 'Destiny? We live to hunt and kill and conquer. What greater destiny is there?'

'But we could be so much more. Why do you refuse to acknowledge that?' They had had this argument before, many times, but Toch'Lu was desperate to make him understand. 'We, alone in the universe, have the power to shape our physical form, yet we are capricious, fickle, adopting attributes such as these wings on a whim, because they delight us. It is time we used our ability to discover our ultimate form, the physical embodiment of everything the gods created us to be.'

'Do not presume to lecture me on the will of the gods. I am the Esteemed Father, Guardian of the Faith, the twelfth-born of the twelfth-born, as it ever shall be, as it ever was. I am the servant of the gods. I am the destiny of the Krillitanes.'

'You are blinded by dogma and enthralled by your own self-importance,' the Brood Mother retorted. 'Your time has passed, cousin. The Krillitanes must follow a new path.'

'And you would lead them?' The Esteemed Father made no attempt to hide his disdain, but there was a wildness in Toch'Lu's gaze that unsettled him, a look of ideological fervour.

'Still you do not understand. My followers and I have no interest in personal gain, or the attainment of power. We merely wish to shepherd the Krillitane race in its endeavour to reach our fullest potential. The destiny of the Krillitanes is not to serve the gods, but to replace them.'

'As the embodiment of the will of the ancient gods, I

cannot allow that.' For the first time there was no malice in the Esteemed Father's tone, just a dry, unequivocal statement of fact.

'Then it is your time to die,' hissed Toch'Lu, and with a screech of fury she launched herself at her adversary, bringing both of them crashing onto the tiles.

Clawing and biting, the combatants bounced across the roof, rolling down towards the edge. Toch'Lu continued her frenzied attack as they tumbled, oblivious to the vicious blows the Esteemed Father dealt her. She was determined to pull him over the edge, even though the fall would certainly kill them both. Her life was unimportant. She would face her final judgement secure in the knowledge that she had sent the Krillitanes upon the path of progress.

Realising her plan, the Esteemed Father abandoned any effort to defend himself and instead scrabbled to grab hold of something, anything that would halt their descent. Tiles splintered as his claws tore through them, but he was powerless to halt their inexorable descent. As the world spun around him he saw it was too late, and they shot over the edge, falling, plummeting downwards.

With a wrench, sudden pain shot through the Esteemed Father's shoulder, ripping through muscles and tendons like jagged glass. By some miracle, their fall had been interrupted.

Toch'Lu hung from his waist, the claws of one hand digging into the flesh above his hip. He looked upwards, ignoring the agony, curious as to who had saved him.

Broken Wing returned his gaze, then looked towards Toch'Lu. Her face was calm, at peace, ready. It was time. The Krillitane released his grip on the Cathedral's stone facade, and the three of them fell, together.

SIXTEEN

The Krillitanes spread across the city like a virulent plague, a torrent of grey-brown bodies crawling through every gap, every possible hiding place in their hunt for the traitor. They moved northwards at speed, through empty houses where breakfasts had been left on tables, fires still burning in hearths, until they caught up with the stragglers, the old and the weak, those unable to flee in time. Then the Krillitanes feasted.

There was little Butcher and his men could do to help, except carry out their orders to evacuate, but the panic spread too quickly for the soldiers to contain it, and the streets flooded with screaming people, running wildly, praying, or simply falling to their knees, waiting for the hounds of hell to drag them into the underworld.

Butcher came to an inn, recognising it as one where

he had spent more than a few bawdy evenings. He tried the door, but it was locked. The publican was a good man, but his wife was a stubborn sort. He'd wager she wouldn't want to leave. 'John, are you in there? Open up. You must leave at once. Your lives are in danger.'

John Garrud's muffled voice came from the other side. 'We aren't going anywhere. Leave us alone.'

The soldier looked back along the street. The Captain's plan had stalled the progress of these dastardly invaders as long as it could, but now all was lost. If he could just save this one last household... 'You'll die if you don't come with me right now.' But his pleas were met with stoic silence.

He heard a disturbance, the clatter of pots and pans being thrown aside, back along the street in a house he had already checked was clear. They were close. Too close for him to escape. Butcher unsheathed his sword, resolving to make a stand. He didn't have to wait long.

Two of the ugly trolls sprang lightly from the shadows of an alley. It was the first time Butcher had seen them up close, and the sight filled him with dread. They sized him up, barking at each other, then the first leapt at him with a hiss. The soldier ducked to one side, bringing down his sword and burying its blade deep in the beast's skull.

The second was on him almost instantly, fangs locked around the forearm he'd instinctively raised to protect himself. His mail armour and leather jerkin offered scant protection as the teeth tore through to the bone, and Butcher screamed out.

'Leave off him, you horrible brute,' shouted John Garrud, storming out of the inn wielding a heavy iron poker, its tip glowing red hot. He swung it at the Krillitane with all the force he could muster and heard the sickening sound of bone caving in. The creature slumped over, and John grabbed Butcher, dragging him back inside as three more Krillitanes bounded up the street.

Before there was time to bolt the door, a Krillitane forced its head through, trying to push it open, but the monster hadn't counted on Gertrude and her candlestick. 'You get out of my inn this instant, or so help me…' she screamed, belting it about the snout repeatedly. 'You're barred. All of you.'

The battered alien whimpered, pulling back, and John slammed the door shut, bolting it and barricading it with an oak table for good measure.

Laying down the poker, he knelt beside the wounded soldier and propped him up, trying to get a look at the poor soul's bleeding arm, which Butcher was clutching close to his chest.

'Are you all right? What the 'ell is going on out there? Demons and brimstone? It ain't normal.'

Gertrude hurried over with a bowl of water and some torn cloth, and began to dress Butcher's damaged arm. 'Leave him be, John, he's hurt.'

'No, they're not demons, John. The Captain told me,' Butcher rambled. 'They're allies of Matilda, come to steal the throne of England. That Doctor fellow seemed to know all about them.'

'Doctor?' Gertrude sucked her teeth, as if she'd expected as much. 'I should have known all this was something to do with him. He's barred and all.'

Something outside crashed against the door. The Krillitanes were trying to smash their way in, and all three humans looked towards it, listening to the hungry squeals clearly audible beyond.

John touched his wife's arm, and said calmly, 'Come on, Gert, it isn't safe here no more. We have to go.'

Gertrude nodded, resolute and determined despite the tear in her eye. 'They'd better not be here when I get back,' she sniffed, and together they lifted Butcher and made their way to the back entrance.

Without anyone at the controls, the skiff had slowed to a halt, floating a little above the water and drifting gently towards the river bank.

Henk looked down at the irritating man lying on the deck. It was about time the Doctor got what was coming to him. 'I'm sure I'm not the first to say this, Doctor, but you really are a total pain in the—'

He didn't get the chance to say any more, as white light exploded violently behind his eyes. Darkness flooded through his senses and he crumpled to the deck, unconscious. Behind him, clutching the maintenance clamp she'd just smashed into the back of his head, stood Emily.

She smiled at the Doctor. 'Who was rescuing who there, exactly?'

'Let's call it quits.' The Doctor grinned, leaping to his feet and giving her an enormous hug. 'Better get him tied up.'

While Emily quickly secured Henk, the Doctor examined the skiff's payload of barrels.

'What are you planning?' Emily asked, watching him skip from barrel to barrel.

'Have you ever heard of crop dusting? It's a method of controlling insect infestations on agricultural farm land. A plane flies in low over the crops, and literally dusts them with insecticide. Think of the Krillitanes as your insects and their oil as—'

'Insecticide,' Emily interrupted, shocked at what the Doctor was suggesting. 'But didn't you say that makes them explode? How is that any less cruel than what Henk was doing?'

'The Krillitanes won't stop once they've found Toch'Lu. They won't leave Earth until they've hunted down every living thing, tasted all it has to offer and taken whatever they want. They'll leave it a barren wasteland, so it's them or a million million species. I've got no choice.' The Doctor looked haunted, as if this course of action were in some way a failure on his part, and Emily understood he didn't take it lightly.

'Besides, hopefully it won't come to that. I've got a plan.' The Doctor had a mischievous glint in his eyes, all hint of worry gone. 'There used to be this TV show, well, there will be this TV show, called *One Man and his Dog*. Sort of like an assault course for sheepdogs and farmers.

Well, I always thought I'd be pretty good at it, and now I'm going to have a chance to find out. We fly this thing over the city walls and spray them with oil. That should put the wind up any stray Krillitanes, and stop them moving any further. Then we'll move inwards…'

Emily grinned, understanding. 'Shepherding the Krillitanes back towards their ship. Brilliant.'

'Isn't it? I wonder what kind of altitude we can get in this thing?' The Doctor became animated again, hurrying over to the skiff's controls. He checked some readings, and then yanked open an access panel. Pulling out a circuit board, he started making adjustments with the sonic screwdriver. 'Not high enough. I'll have to override the safety compensators. There.'

Replacing the circuit board, the Doctor threw himself into the pilot's chair and began to flick switches, ramping up the power to the engines. He winked at Emily, and smiled a wild, excited smile. 'I'd hang on to something if I were you. This is going to get hairy.'

'What in heaven's name is that?' Miller exclaimed in a hushed voice. 'A dragon? Where did Matilda get a dragon?'

'She must've sold her soul to Beelzebub, God help us,' whispered another of the men.

Darke gazed upon Henk's creation in wonder, spellbound by its majestic, deadly beauty. It was a dragon, there was no other word to describe it. The stuff of legends. As if the other Krillitanes hadn't been terrible enough, they now seemed like lambs compared to this monumental beast.

Having smashed its way through the Chapter House door, the Krillitane Storm had found itself alone in the cloisters garden, feeling the fresh air against its skin for the first time in many months. Almost joyfully, the huge animal had lifted itself from the ground with elegant, languid strokes of its enormous wings.

Darke's men had looked on in astonishment as the thing had appeared from behind the Cathedral, landing almost delicately amidst the snow and dead bodies.

That it should fall to him and a handful of his beleaguered men to confront this awe-inspiring creature of mythical proportions! It was absurd, impossible. But confront it they must.

'Form a perimeter,' Darke instructed, betraying no hint of the fear that burned in his stomach. 'Surround the animal and move forwards. It can't take us all on.'

Some perimeter, he thought. Half a dozen tired, brave men against that thing. The dragon's head swung this way and that, tracking the movement of the troops as they took up positions along its flanks and to its rear, barking and snapping at them, wary but unsure of their purpose.

'Go for the legs, at the joints, and damage the wings if you can. Even the odds,' the Captain shouted. He shook his shoulders to release some tension, checked the weight and balance of his sword, and gritted his teeth. Nothing for it, they had to bring it down.

'Charge!' Darke roared, and stormed headlong at the beast.

Howling, it reared up on its hind legs, and flicked its muscular tail, swatting Miller and another soldier away as if they were buzzing mosquitoes. No time to worry about them. Darke leapt out of the way, as the dragon's hand-like paws pummelled into the ground, its bony fingers digging into the earth. He took a mighty swing with his sword, aiming for a fleshy area between its thumb and forefinger. The blade sliced deep, and immediately the beast reared up again, bellowing in pain. The Captain lost grip of his sword, which remained lodged in the wound and was swept away, high out of his reach.

Darke didn't have long to worry about being defenceless, as the abomination plucked him from the ground with its good paw, lifting him towards its open mouth where row upon row of jagged teeth, dripping with saliva, were waiting to tear him to shreds.

On the ground, the remaining men fought ever harder, spurred on by the predicament of their commander, drawing the dragon's focus away from Darke and forcing it to concentrate on fending off their barrage of attacks.

The Captain gasped as the creature's grip tightened around his chest, a crushing pressure that was almost too much to bear. Without a weapon, there was nothing he could do to help his men, and he watched in horror as another was crushed beneath the dragon's heel.

Then he remembered the small glass tube the Doctor had entrusted to him, the special liquid possessed of miraculous properties, which he'd placed in his belt pouch for safe keeping. What was it the Doctor had said? The oil was a poison to the Krillitane, a blessing and a curse. A curse...

Did he have enough faith left in him to trust in some superstitious notion of a curse, a magic potion? The Doctor had considered it powerful enough, and spoke of the liquid's properties as something real, tangible, lethal. With no sword, the Captain needed an alternative weapon. He would put his faith in the Doctor. He had faith in the Doctor.

Darke reached for the leather pouch on his belt, his fingertips brushing against it. The dragon was again lifting him towards its mouth. He had but moments. Straining, his fingers finally gripped the glass tube, pulled it from the pouch. His face was so close to the yellow fangs...

He threw the tube hard, as hard as he could manage.

The test tube shattered against an enormous canine, splattering oil extract across the monster's gums and tongue, and Darke suddenly found himself falling.

For a moment he blacked out, but the freezing snow against his face brought him round with a start. Darke rolled onto his back and stared up at the dragon. It was blinking, mouth flapping as if it had a bad taste in its mouth. Then it began to twitch and stagger unnaturally, scratching wildly at its mouth, seemingly unaware that it was slashing into its own face with its claws. And all the while its body was changing, hideous, anachronous mutations rippling across its flesh, through its bones, as the oil extract aggressively attacked its DNA, forcing random evolutionary changes at an unsustainable rate.

The beast let out an ungodly whine, arched its back, and crashed heavily to the ground, body wracked with convulsions, pustules bubbling across its skin. With one last great shudder, it whimpered and died.

Butcher was losing blood, despite Gertrude's hastily applied dressing, and the trail of crimson they had left in the snow was drawing more Krillitanes towards them.

'Leave me here. I'll be all right,' Butcher mumbled, his voice was hoarse and cracked.

'Don't be such a turnip and carry on walking.' John wasn't having any of that kind of talk.

'I knew we should have stayed in the inn. We could've hidden in the cellar, they'd never have found us,' Gertrude complained, more to blot out the grimmer thoughts that were occupying her mind than in actual belief they would have been safe anywhere.

'We'll be at the wall soon. Someone there will help.' John was breathing heavily, supporting the injured soldier as best he could. 'Keep moving, Gert. They aren't far behind us.'

Gertrude rolled her eyes. 'Are they not? Well that is a shock and a half. You never know, hopefully we'll bump into the Devil's Huntsman and we can all have a party.'

There was a blur of movement ahead of them, and Gertrude screamed as a Krillitane appeared out of nowhere, then another. In seconds they were surrounded, the beasts hissing and closing in around them. They were done for.

'Gert, old girl, I'm only going to say this the once, so don't think I'll be making a habit of it,' John said, as the three of them huddled closer, waiting for the first monster to strike.

'You don't have to say anything, John,' Gertrude interrupted. 'I know.' She smiled warmly at her husband. It didn't happen often, but it melted his old heart every time.

'S'pose not.' He smiled back, oblivious to the growl of the Krillitane nearest to them. It crouched low, ready to feast.

Without warning, a thunderclap exploded above their heads, and a shape flashed across the sky. In the same instant they found themselves drenched in a sticky, wet fluid.

'What in blazes...?' exclaimed John, tentatively examining the oily substance covering his skin. He sucked his finger. 'Tastes like chicken.'

He looked up to find the beast that had been poised to attack now shuddering, apparently on fire, smoke curling away from its bubbling, boiling flesh. It screamed, an agonising yelp full of fear and pain and shock, and its companions looked on, horrified.

Before John's eyes, the creature evaporated in a blaze of unnatural light, exploding like seed pods bursting open in a meadow, and the remaining beasts fled.

***

'That got 'em!' Emily shouted.

The Doctor banked the skiff to the left, checking to make sure the trio of humans was now safe. He could see pockets of Krillitanes in the streets below, retreating in panic towards the Cathedral, any advance outwards from the city blocked by the oil spraying furiously from the barrels on the skiff. With the perimeter walls and outlying streets bathed in the oil, they had nowhere else to go. The Doctor's plan was working.

'This one's almost empty, and we've only got two more barrels. Is that going to be enough?' Emily shouted above the noise of the skiff's engines. She'd used Henk's blaster to blow a scorched hole into the side of each of the now empty tanks, forcing the pressurised Krillitane Oil to spew out and rain down on the city.

'More than enough,' the Doctor shouted back, satisfied that their task was complete. 'We've covered most of the city, and it looks like any Krillitanes we missed are heading back to their ship.'

'Are we going after them?'

'Only to make sure they leave. All of them.' The Doctor twisted the throttle. The last time he'd seen them, Toch'Lu and the Esteemed Father had been at each other's throats, and the fate of the Earth rested upon which had emerged victorious.

The Doctor set the skiff down, not far from the Chapter House. He noticed three dark shapes in the snow, surrounded by a handful of Krillitanes, who scattered at the noise of the approaching craft. Still more Krillitane stragglers rushed past, ignoring the bodies, desperate to reach their ship.

As Emily and the Doctor approached, it became clear that the nearest shape was the broken body of the Esteemed Father. He was dead, neck bent at a sickening angle, his back shattered in the fall. A few metres away, Broken Wing knelt in the snow, clinging to Toch'Lu's lifeless remains, grieving for the loss of his Brood Mother, his mate.

'I'm sorry,' said the Doctor quietly. 'I'm so sorry.'

Broken Wing lifted his head, fire in his eyes. 'Her death will not be in vain. The Esteemed Father is defeated. I shall gather my Brood, and return home. We have enough supporters at court to set the Krillitane race upon a new path. The path she wished us to take.'

'Well, so long as that path takes the Krillitanes far away from here, that would be a good start.'

The Doctor and Broken Wing stared long and hard at each other, before the Krillitane climbed painfully to his feet, lifting Toch'Lu tenderly in his arms. He limped towards the frigate's boarding ramp, and didn't look back.

SEVENTEEN

'They're gone for good, aren't they?' Emily asked, as the last of the Krillitanes boarded their ship and its ramp retracted into the hull.

'Give it nine hundred years or so and they might try their luck, but no need for you to worry about that. It's already been dealt with.'

Emily frowned and glanced at the Doctor, curiously. There was so much about this man that remained unexplained, mysteries that she imagined few would ever get to the bottom of, as if he'd lived a dozen lives and would live a dozen more, finding a universe of excitement in all of them.

A sudden blast of heat broke through her reverie, accompanied by the roar of retro-thrusters. The Krillitane vessel dragged itself into the air, engaging its main engines and pointing its nose at the heavens. A blaze of light illuminated the thick cloud cover as the frigate broke through them, and soon the raging thunder of its engines became a distant rumble, then silence. One final sonic boom signified it had reached escape velocity.

'That's that, then,' the Doctor sighed, staring into space. He sniffed, and turned to Emily. 'So, what will you do now? Go back to university? Carry on being a big-shot bounty hunter?'

Emily laughed. 'I don't think so. I'm not really cut out for this line of work. Besides, that was Dad's world. Time to make my own way. If nothing else, Henk has left behind a lot of valuable junk. I could probably make a fair bit selling it for scrap. Maybe enough to buy my way back into college.'

'Which leaves us with one knotty little problemo.' The Doctor nodded towards Henk, still bound to the skiff's loading arm, showing no sign of waking.

'Let's call him an unresolved opportunity, shall we? I've had enough of problems.' The young woman smiled, feeling happier than she had done in months.

'He had some pretty high-profile customers in there, you know, and not all of them made it out alive. I reckon he'll have made a few powerful enemies, the Calabrians, the Octulans, and they'll be looking for justice.' The Doctor had a conspiratorial gleam in his eye. 'Who knows, if someone knew where he was, well... They'd be able to demand a pretty high bounty for old Mister Henk.'

Now they both smiled. She'd be all right, he decided, as they made their way to the city side of the Cathedral.

As they wandered out of the main entrance, they immediately saw the remains of the Krillitane Storm, now little more than a pile of smoking bones.

'Doctor. Emily.'

They both looked towards a voice they recognised.

'Captain Darke!' exclaimed the Doctor, joyfully grabbing the soldier's hand. 'Brilliant. Oh, it's brilliant to see you. Was it you finished off this big fella?'

'Not just me, sir. A lot of good men gave their lives in the battle. Mind you, some of the men have already started calling me Saint George.' Darke looked embarrassed. 'Doctor, I'm afraid I broke your glass bottle. Was it terribly valuable?'

'Priceless. To the likes of Mister Henk, anyway.' The Doctor replied, looking serious for a moment, but he couldn't keep it up for long and winked at Darke. 'But if it hasn't got a price then how can it be worth anything, eh?'

By late morning, people had begun streaming through the city gates, going back to their homes and businesses. Already some sense of normality had returned. Henk was now safely locked away in the holding cell on Emily's ship, and contact had been made with the Calabrian government, who were understandably very keen to get their hands on him.

The Doctor had made a point of examining the Sheriff,

who turned out to be a very nice man after all, and would be perfectly fine in time, despite the months spent under Henk's mental control.

Finally, the Doctor, Emily and Captain Darke arrived in an otherwise deserted alley, ignoring the stinking heap of rubbish nearby.

'That's a coincidence. This is exactly the spot one of my Bio-locator Pods malfunctioned. Right where this little blue shed is.' Emily walked up to the tall blue box with the 'Police' sign across the top.

'Really? Sorry about that. Probably my fault,' said the Doctor, reaching past Emily and unlocking the TARDIS door.

Emily looked on in amazement. 'Don't tell me this box is your ship?'

'What? Leave it alone. It's a lovely old thing.' The Doctor pretended to be hurt. He hated goodbyes, and would have much rather taken his leave when they weren't looking. 'Right, time I was off. Captain, it's been an honour. You're a good man, but take it easy for a bit, yeah? Kick back and put your feet up.'

'Whatever you say, Doctor. Not that I ever understand a word you say, but yes, whatever you say.' Darke bowed and stepped discreetly away as the Doctor turned to Emily.

'And as for you, just get yourself back to that university and learn stuff, and pass your exams and have a brilliant life, and…'

'Thanks for everything, Doctor. I'll never forget you,'

Emily said and, before she could stop herself, she held his face and kissed him tenderly. Darke found he was suddenly fascinated by the rats and their pile of rubbish.

'Yes, and… and that too. Well then, bye then.' The Doctor looked flustered, ruffled his hair and grinned broadly. He opened the TARDIS door and ducked inside. A moment later and the lamp on the police box roof began to flash, accompanied by a straining, thumping, thunderous echo, and the strange blue box faded impossibly into nothingness.

'I don't believe it,' Emily whispered.

Darke blinked in astonishment. 'Neither do I. The Doctor's little blue house just disappeared into thin air.'

'No, not that. Look.'

Emily crouched down and picked up a flattened metal disc, all that remained of her malfunctioning Bio-locator Pod, crushed into the ground where the blue box had been standing. She smiled.

'Typical.'

Acknowledgements

I promised I wouldn't cry, but… Oh, hang on, this isn't an awards ceremony, is it? I mean, who do I think I am, Kate Winslet? Anyway…

Huge thanks to Justin Richards, for giving me this chance to take a spin in the Vortex.

Special mention also to Nicholas Payne, my Historical Adviser, without whose input this novel wouldn't have a shred of historical authenticity. Not that there's a great deal of *actual* history in it, but what little there *is* is bang on the money.

I'm also grateful to those whose names I've borrowed to populate this tale. Thanks to Richard Darke for providing the Captain with his very cool surname, and to my good friend Charlie Gee, whose online pseudonym 'Henk Toeclaw' gave me two for the price of one. Anyone else whose name crops up in the text, you know who you are and you should be ashamed of yourselves.

Thanks to Moray, Annie, Paul and everyone else at DWA. Without you chaps, where would I be now, eh? Keep being brilliant.

To Mum, Dad, Steve, Lisa, Holly, Megan, Rosie, Jack and (at the time of writing) the as yet unnamed fifth element, thanks so much for your love and support.

Finally, and most especially, this book is for my beautiful daughter, Emily. (Come on, you didn't think I'd name my guest companion at random, did you? Imagine the brownie points I'll score once Emily is old enough to read this!)

At the heart of the ruined city of Arcopolis is the Fortress.
It's a brutal structure placed here by one of the sides in
a devastating intergalactic war that's long ended. Fifteen
years ago, the entire population of the planet was killed in
an instant by the weapon housed deep in the heart of the
Fortress. Now only the ghosts remain.

The Doctor arrives, and determines to fight his way
past the Fortress's automatic defences and put the
weapon beyond use. But he soon discovers he's not the
only person in Arcopolis. What is the true nature of
the weapon? Is the planet really haunted? Who are the
Eyeless? And what will happen if they get to the weapon
before the Doctor?

The Doctor has a fight on his hands. And this time he's all
on his own.

◄ DOCTOR · WHO ►

Judgement of the Judoon
by Colin Brake
ISBN 978 1 846 07639 8
£6.99

Elvis the King Spaceport has grown into the sprawling
city-state of New Memphis – an urban jungle, where
organised crime is rife. But the launch of the new
Terminal 13 hasn't been as smooth as expected. And
things are about to get worse...

When the Doctor arrives, he finds the whole terminal
locked down. The notorious Invisible Assassin is at work
again, and the Judoon troopers sent to catch him will stop
at nothing to complete their mission.

With the assassin loose on the mean streets of New
Memphis, the Doctor is forced into a strange alliance.
Together with teenage private eye Nikki and a ruthless
Judoon Commander, the Doctor soon discovers that
things are even more complicated – and dangerous – than
he first thought…

DOCTOR·WHO

The Slitheen Excursion

by Simon Guerrier

ISBN 978 1 846 07640 4

£6.99

1500BC – King Actaeus and his subjects live in mortal fear of the awesome gods who have come to visit their kingdom in ancient Greece. Except the Doctor, visiting with university student June, knows they're not gods at all. They're aliens.

For the aliens, it's the perfect holiday – they get to tour the sights of a primitive planet and even take part in local customs. Like gladiatorial games, or hunting down and killing humans who won't be missed.

With June's enthusiastic help, the Doctor soon meets the travel agents behind this deadly package holiday company – his old enemies the Slitheen. But can he bring the Slitheen excursion to an end without endangering more lives? And how are events in ancient Greece linked to a modern-day alien plot to destroy what's left of the Parthenon?

DOCTOR·WHO

The Taking of Chelsea 426
by David Llewellyn
ISBN 978 1 846 07758 6
£6.99

The Chelsea Flower Show – hardly the most exciting or
dangerous event in the calendar, or so the Doctor thinks.
But this is Chelsea 426, a city-sized future colony floating
on the clouds of Saturn, and the flowers are much more
than they seem.

As the Doctor investigates, he becomes more and more
worried. Why is shopkeeper Mr Pemberton acting so
strangely? And what is Professor Wilberforce's terrible
secret?

They are close to finding the answers when a familiar foe
arrives, and the stakes suddenly get much higher. The
Sontarans have plans of their own, and they're not here to
arrange flowers…

◆ DOCTOR · WHO ◆

Autonomy
by Daniel Blythe
ISBN 978 1 846 07759 3
£6.99

Hyperville is 2013's top high-tech 24-hour entertainment
complex – a sprawling palace of fun under one massive
roof. You can go shopping, or experience the excitement
of Doomcastle, WinterZone or Wild West World.
But things are about to get a lot more exciting – and
dangerous...

What unspeakable horror is lurking on Level Zero of
Hyperville? And what will happen when the entire
complex goes over to Central Computer Control?

For years, the Nestene Consciousness has been waiting
and planning, recovering from its wounds. But now
it's ready, and its deadly plastic Autons are already in
place around the complex. Now more than ever, visiting
Hyperville will be an unforgettable experience...

DOCTOR·WHO

The Ultimate Monster Guide

by Justin Richards

ISBN 978 1 846 07745 6

£15.99

With *The Ultimate Monster Guide*, *Doctor Who* historian Justin Richards has created the most comprehensive guide to the Doctor's enemies ever published. With fully illustrated entries that cover everything from Adipose and Autons to Zarbi and Zygons, this guide tells you everything you need to know about the many dastardly creatures the Doctor has fought since he first appeared on television.

Featuring a wealth of material from the current and classic series, the guide also includes behind-the-scenes secrets of how the monsters were created, as well as design drawings and images. Find out how the Cybermen were redesigned over the years, and how Davros was resurrected to lead his Daleks once again. Discover the computer magic that made the Beast possible, and the make-up wizardry that created the Weeping Angels. Learn how many incarnations of the Master the Doctor has encountered, and which other misguided Time Lords he has defeated…

Lavishly designed with photos and artwork throughout, *The Ultimate Monster Guide* is essential reading for all travellers in time and space!